Chick and Brain
Smell my Foot!

Cece Bell

CANDLEWICK PRESS

CONTENTS

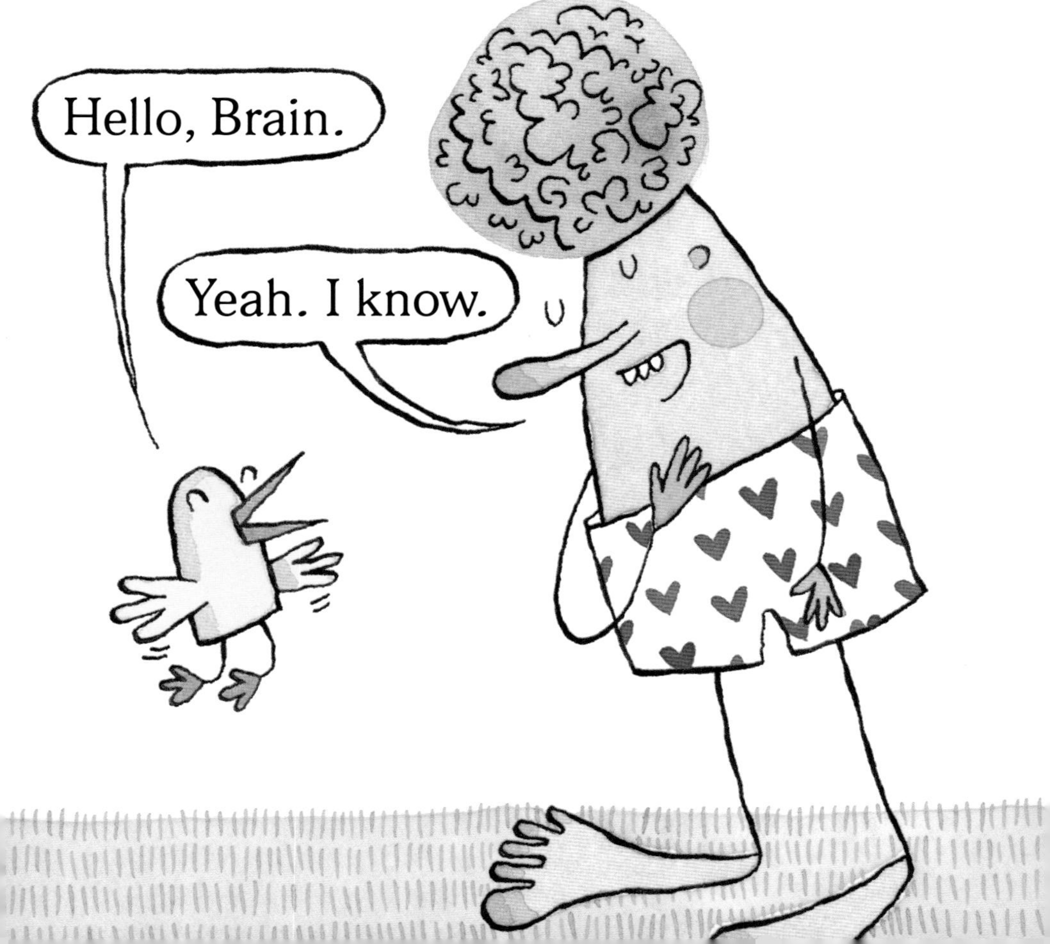
Hello, Brain.
Yeah. I know.

Chapter 1

Foot

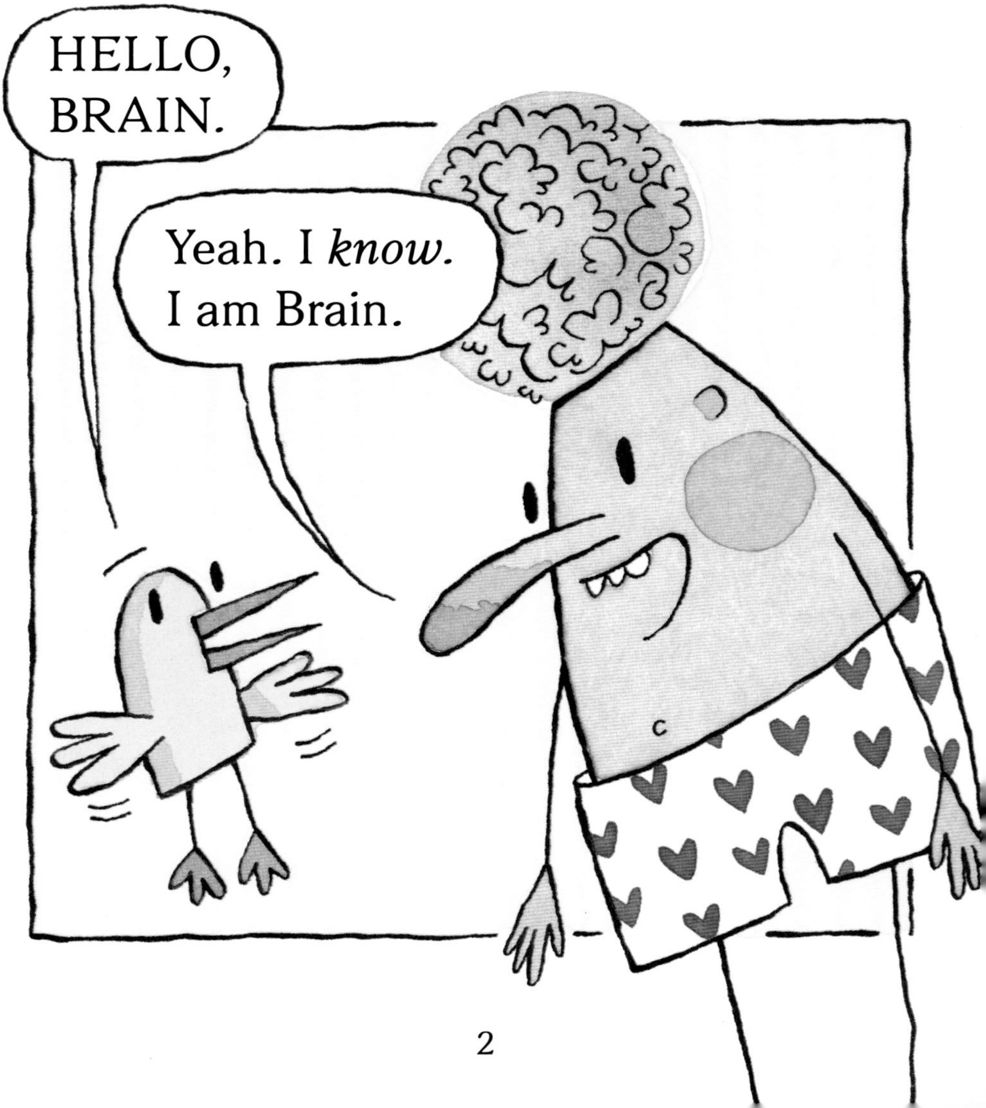
HELLO, BRAIN.
Yeah. I *know.* I am Brain.

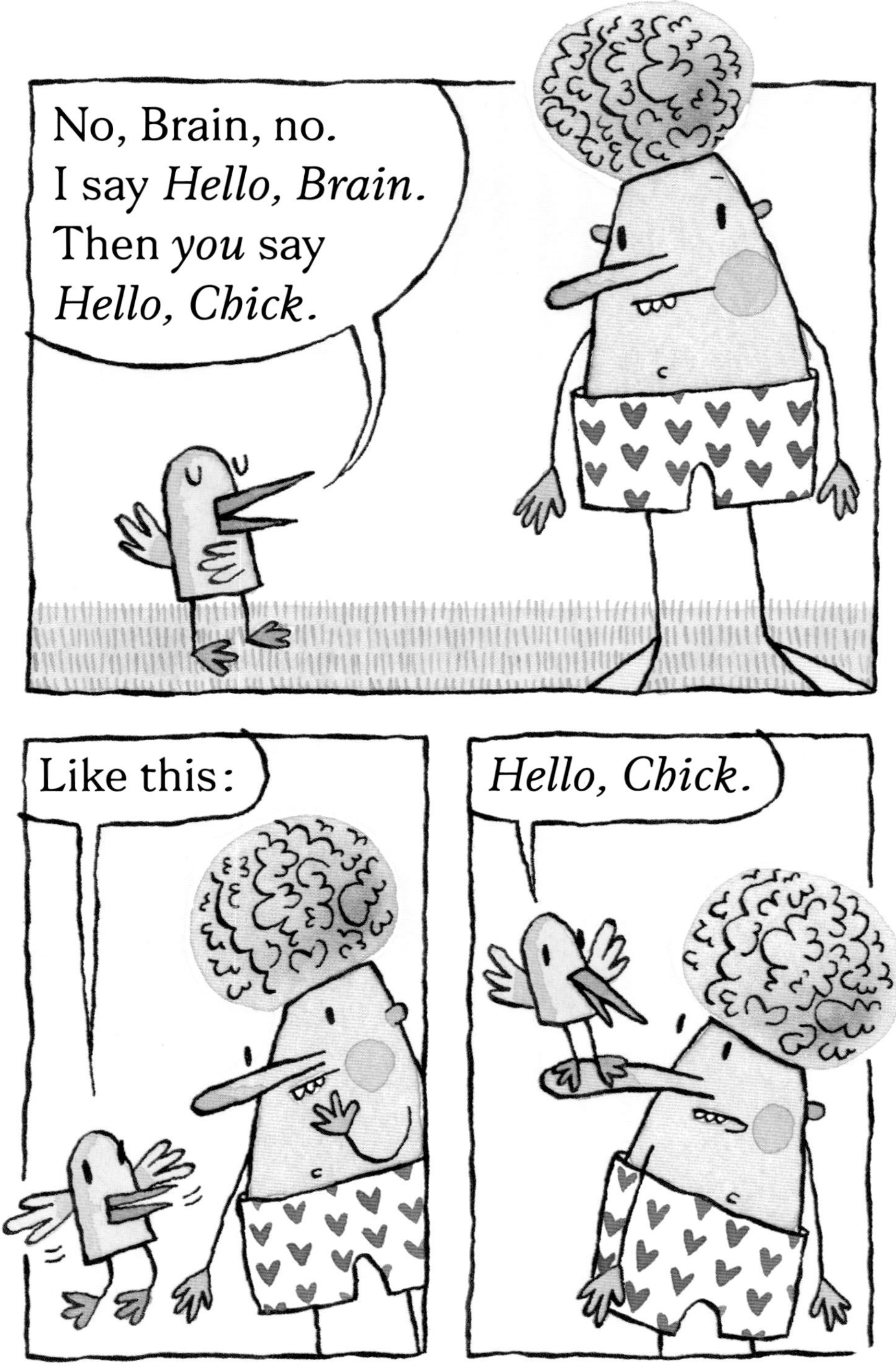
No, Brain, no.
I say *Hello, Brain.*
Then *you* say
Hello, Chick.
Like this:
Hello, Chick.

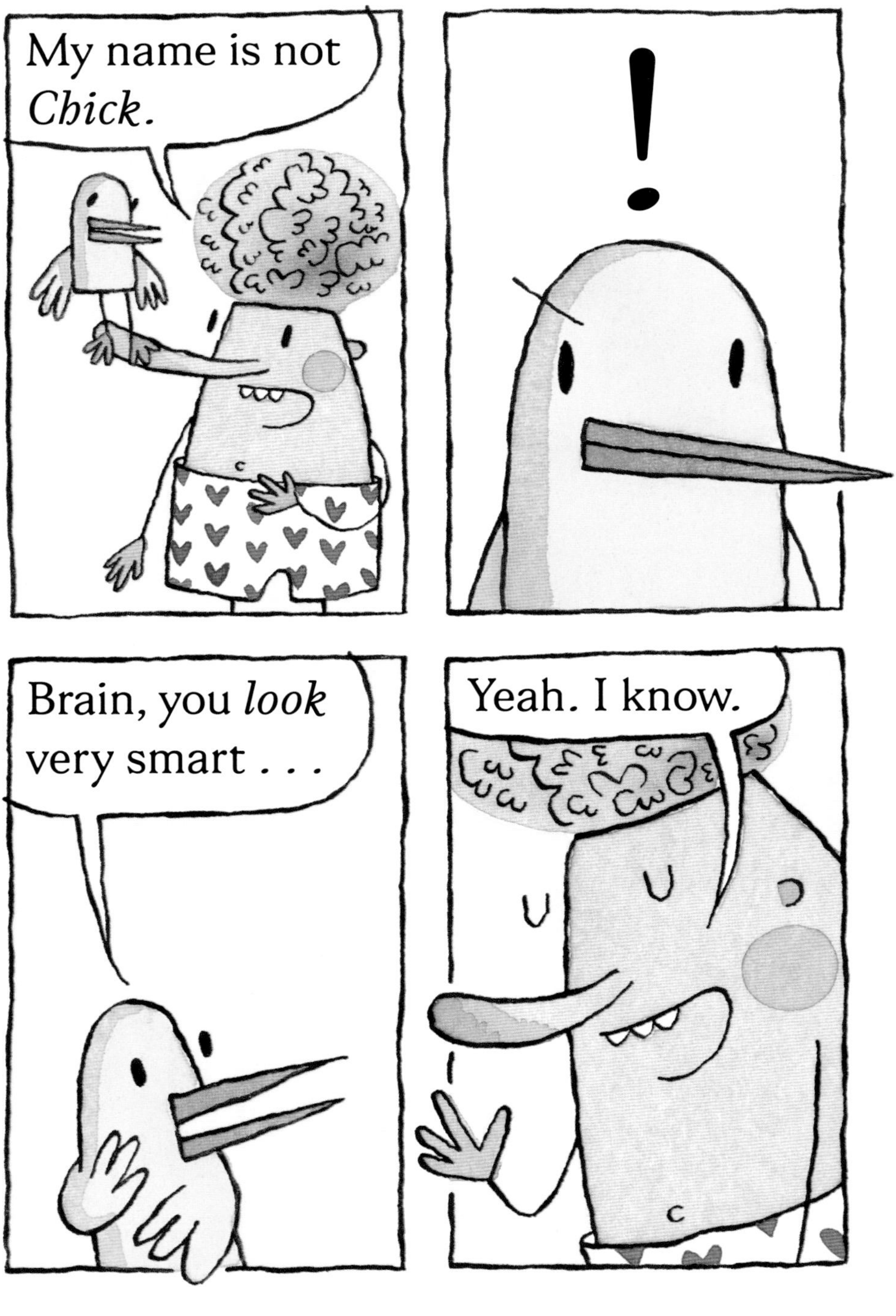
My name is not *Chick*.
!
Brain, you *look* very smart . . .
Yeah. I know.

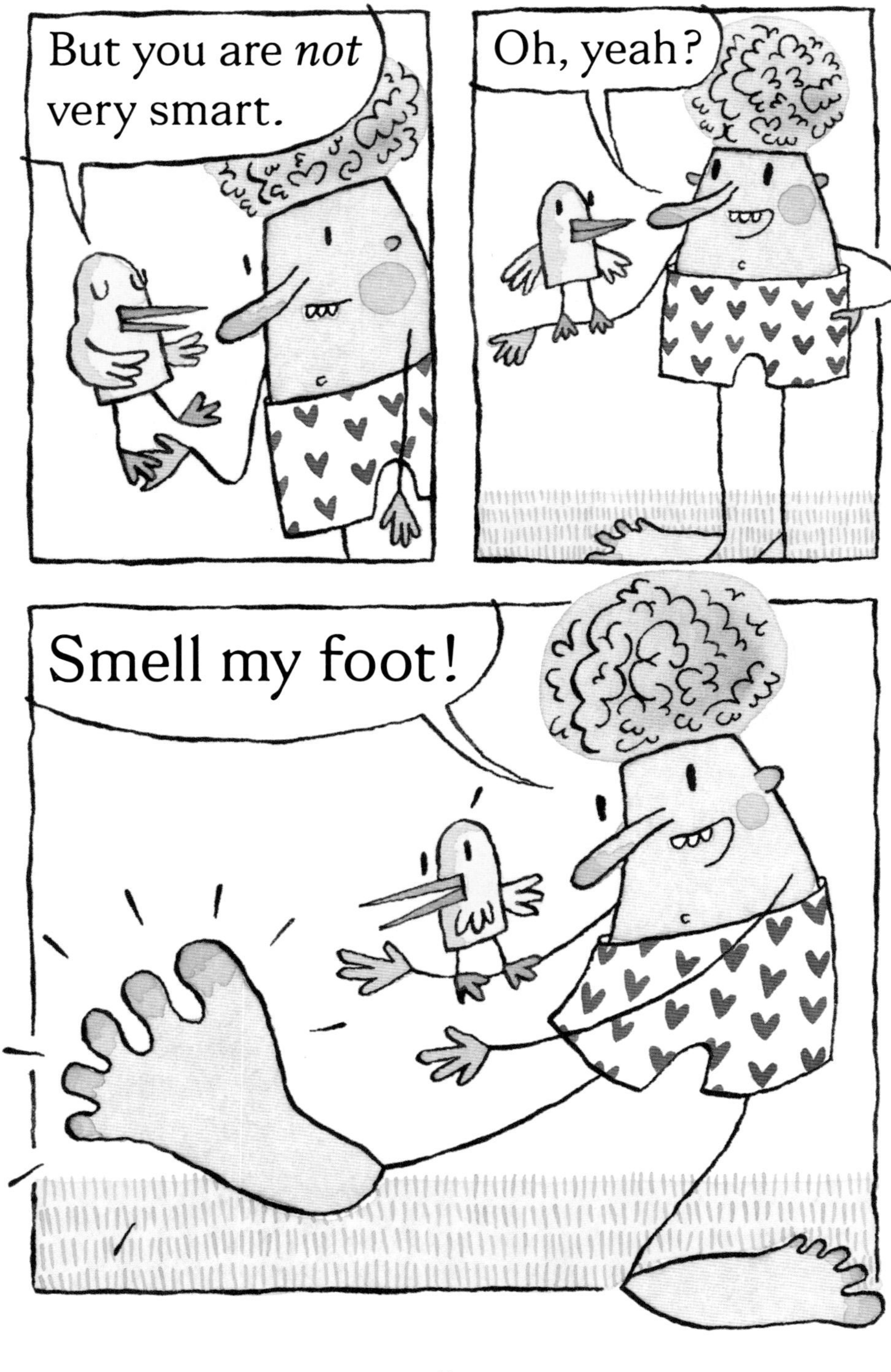
But you are *not* very smart.
Oh, yeah?
Smell my foot!

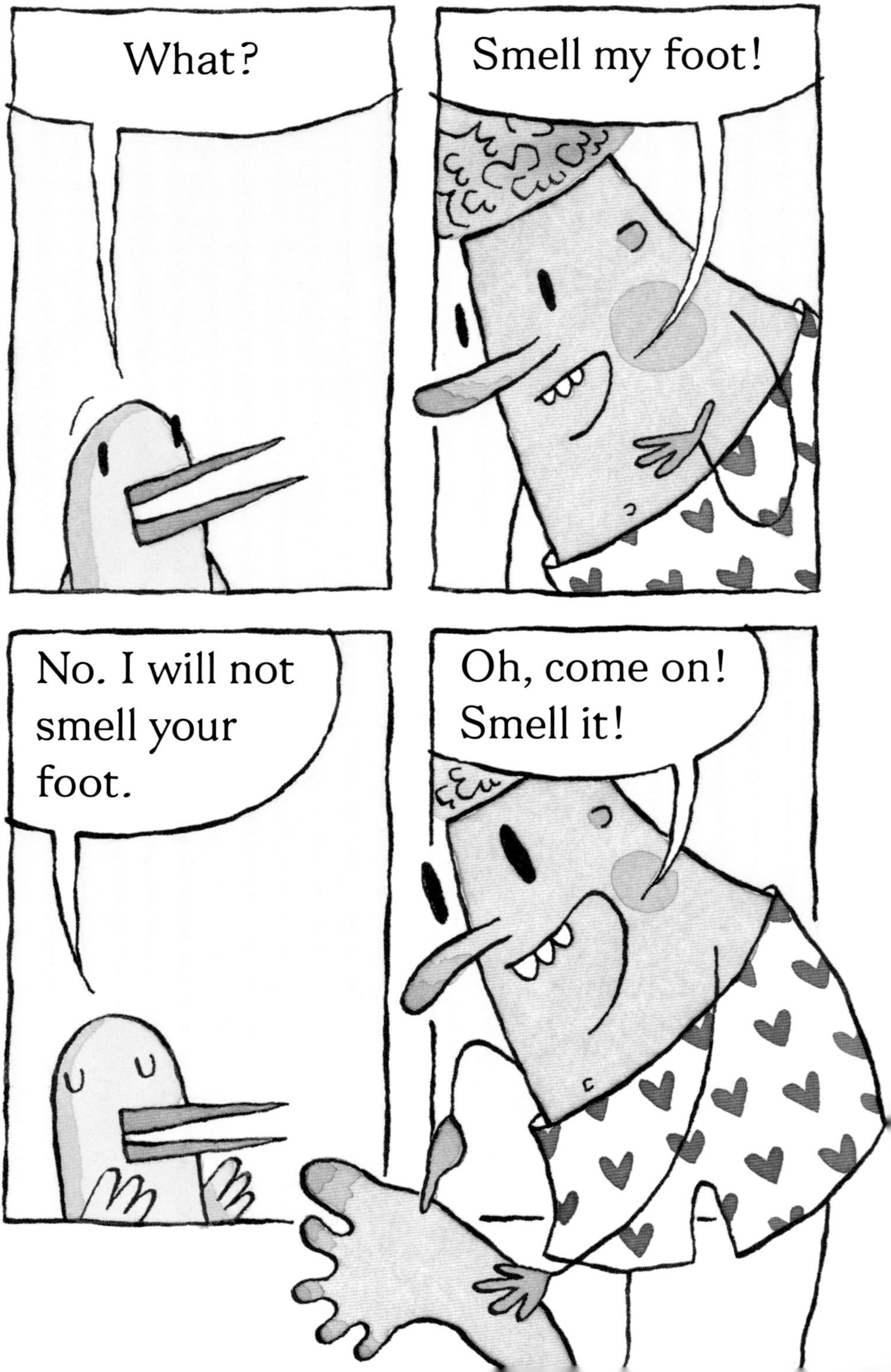
What?
Smell my foot!
No. I will not smell your foot.
Oh, come on! Smell it!

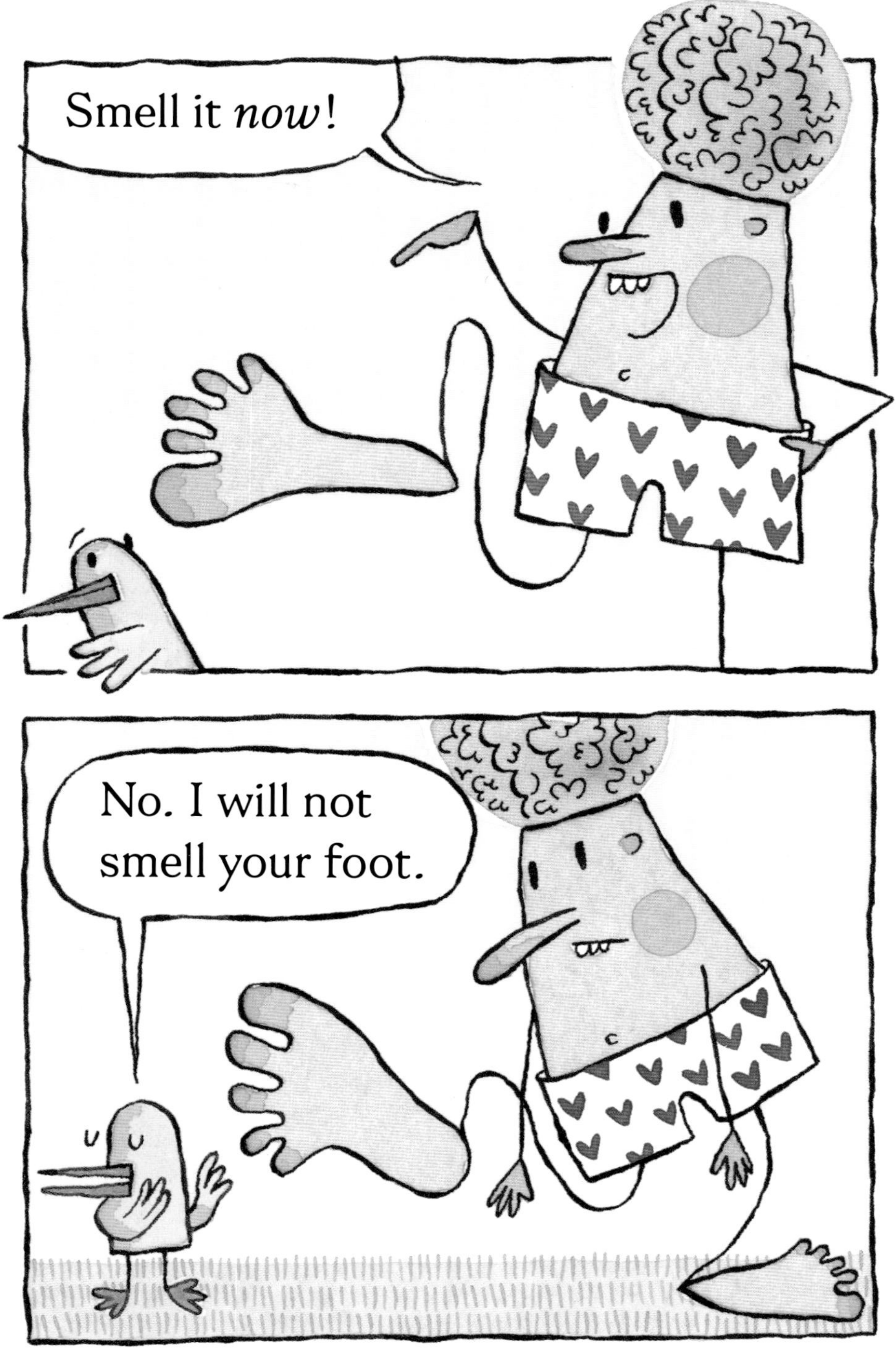
Smell it *now*!
No. I will not smell your foot.

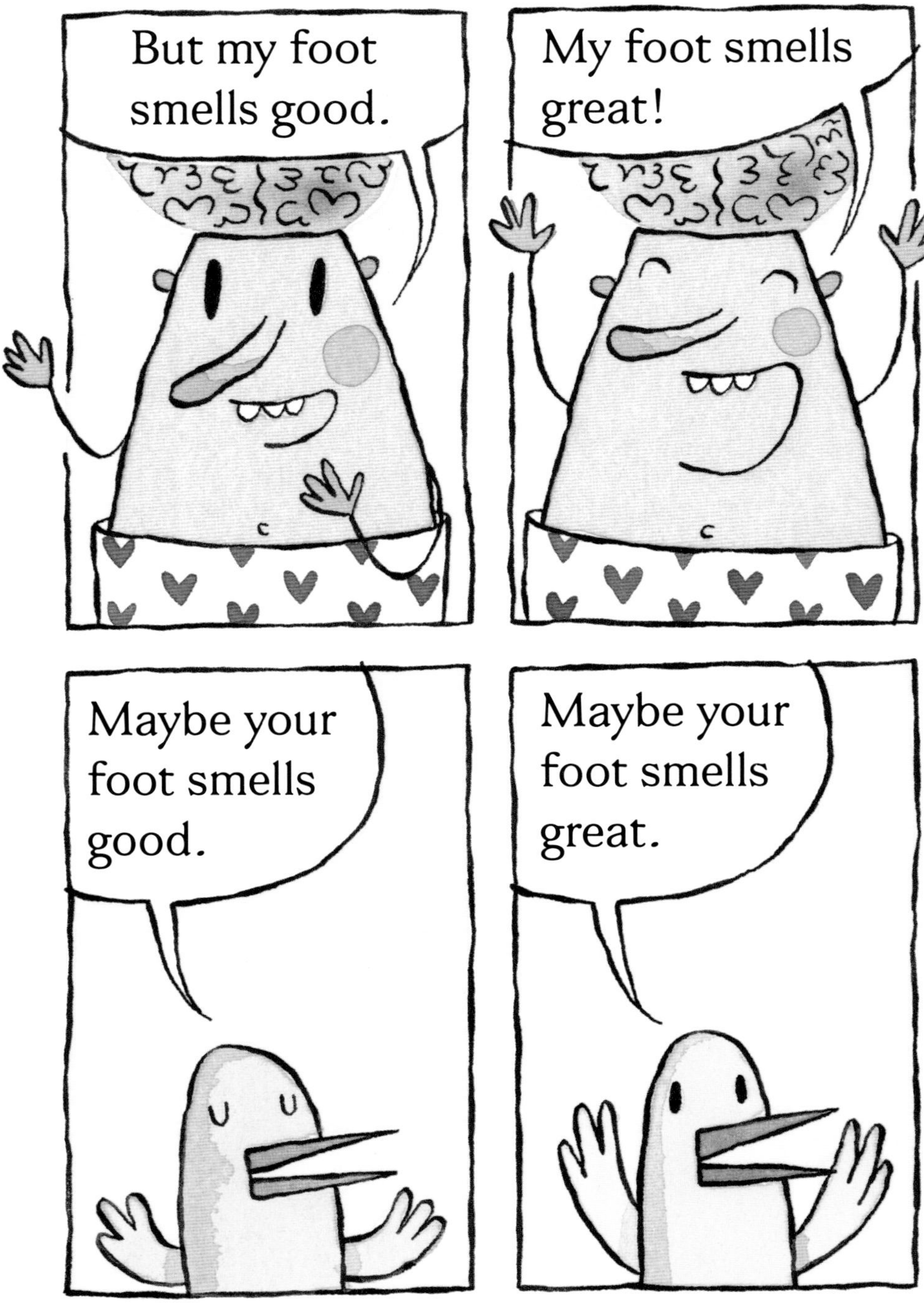
But my foot smells good.
My foot smells great!
Maybe your foot smells good.
Maybe your foot smells great.

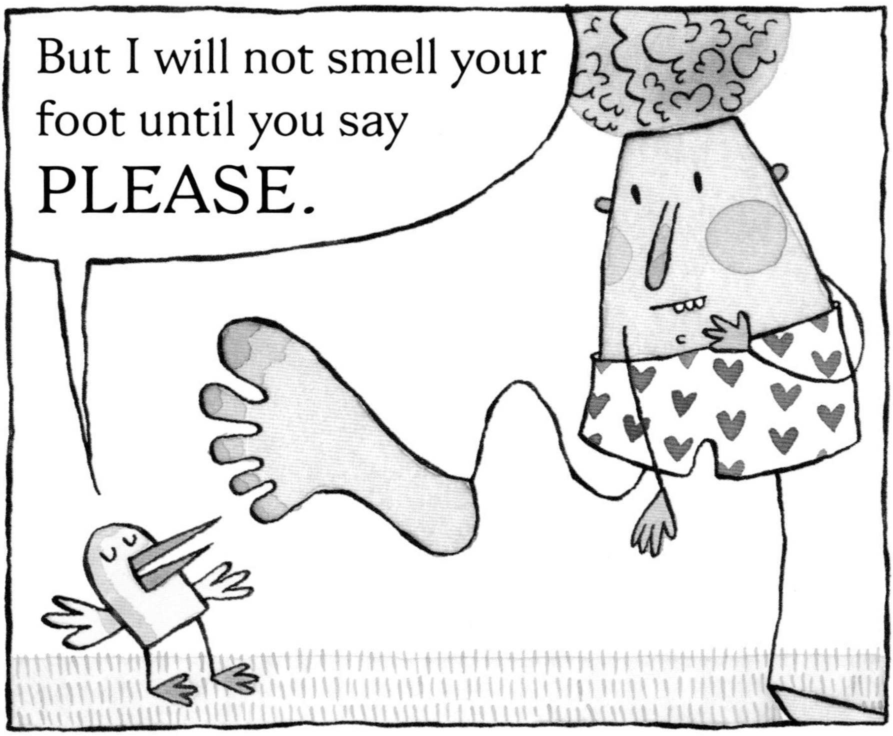
But I will not smell your foot until you say PLEASE.

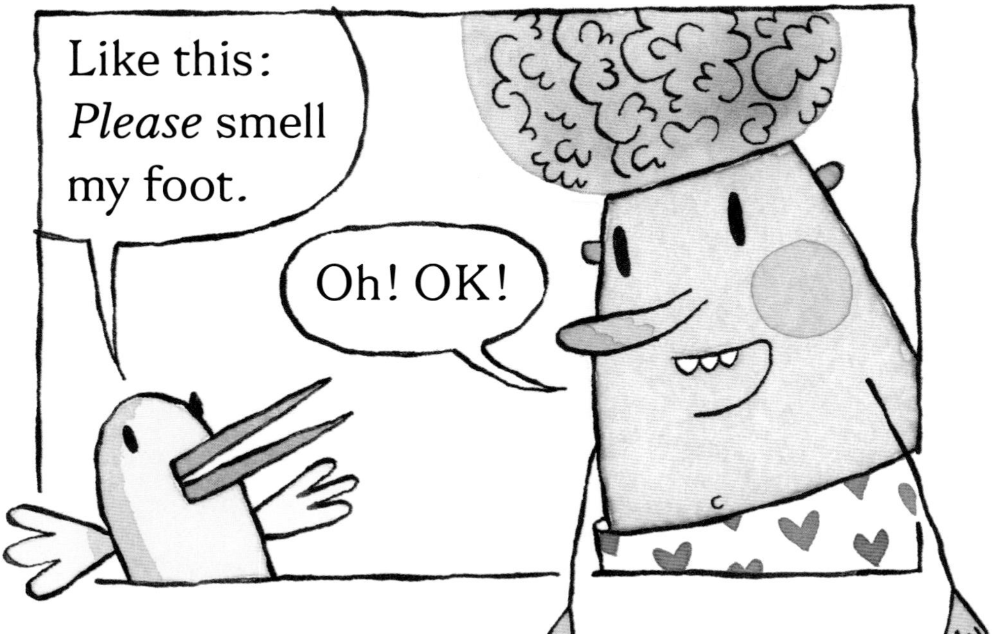
Like this: *Please* smell my foot.
Oh! OK!

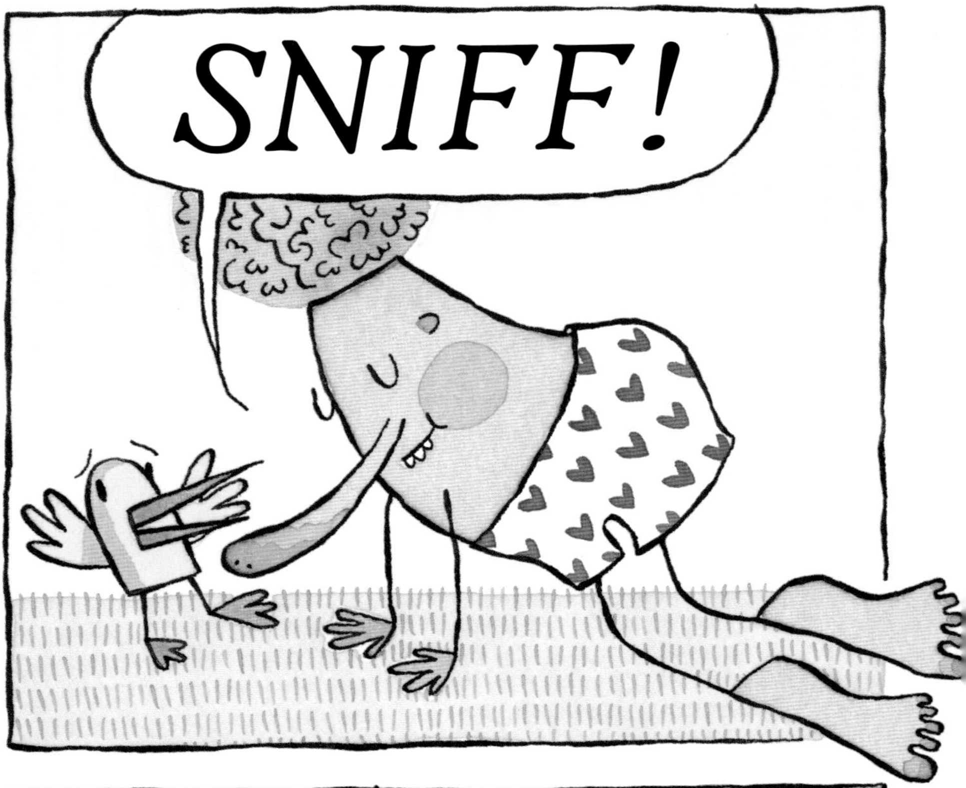
SNIFF!

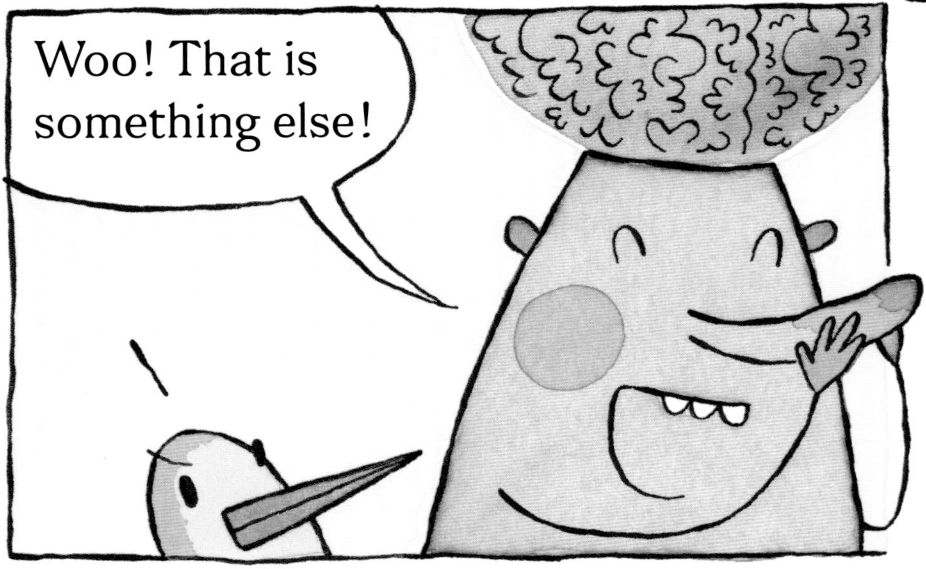
Woo! That is something else!

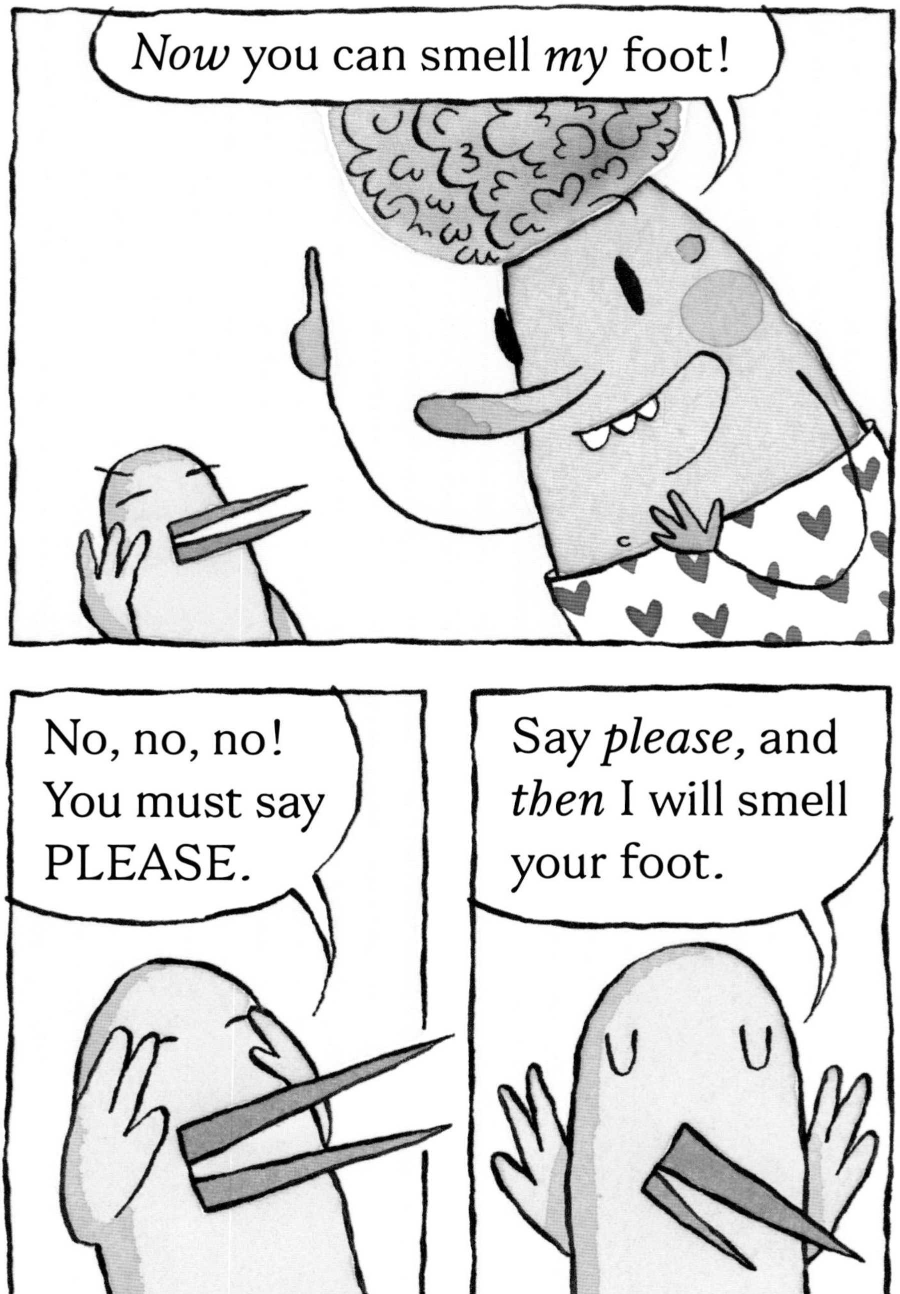
Now you can smell *my* foot!
No, no, no! You must say PLEASE.
Say *please,* and *then* I will smell your foot.

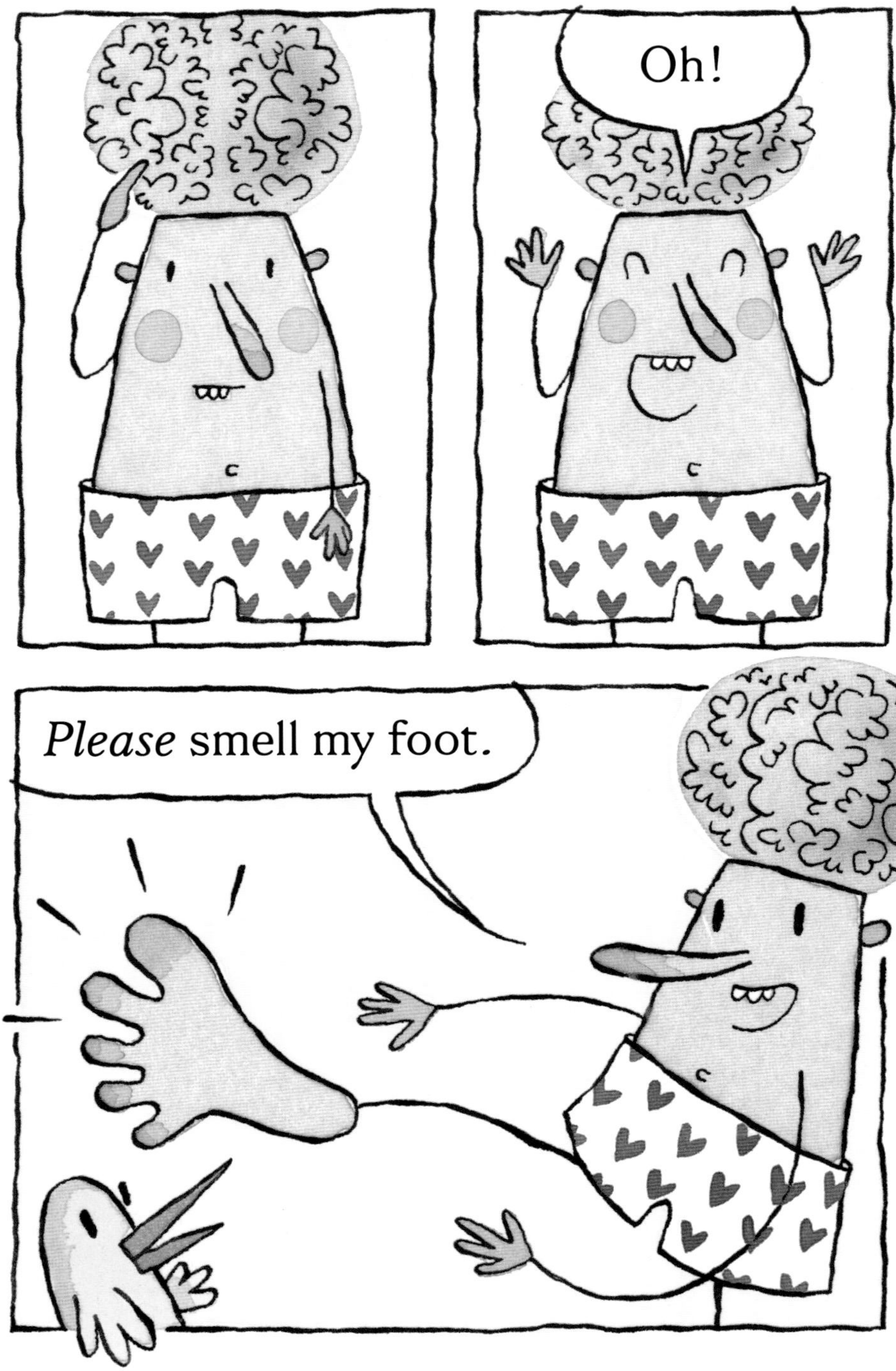
Oh!
Please smell my foot.

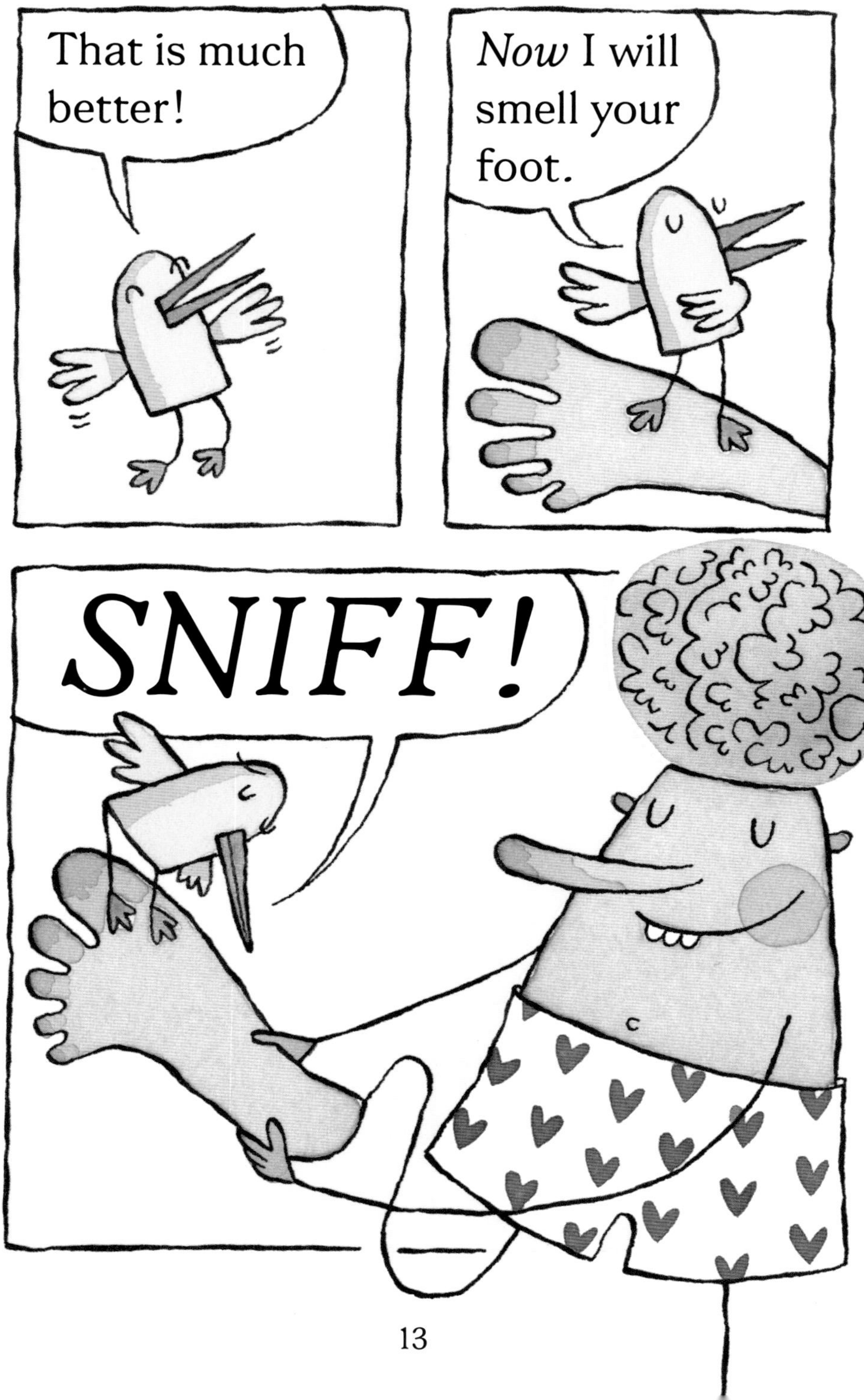
That is much better!
Now I will smell your foot.
SNIFF!

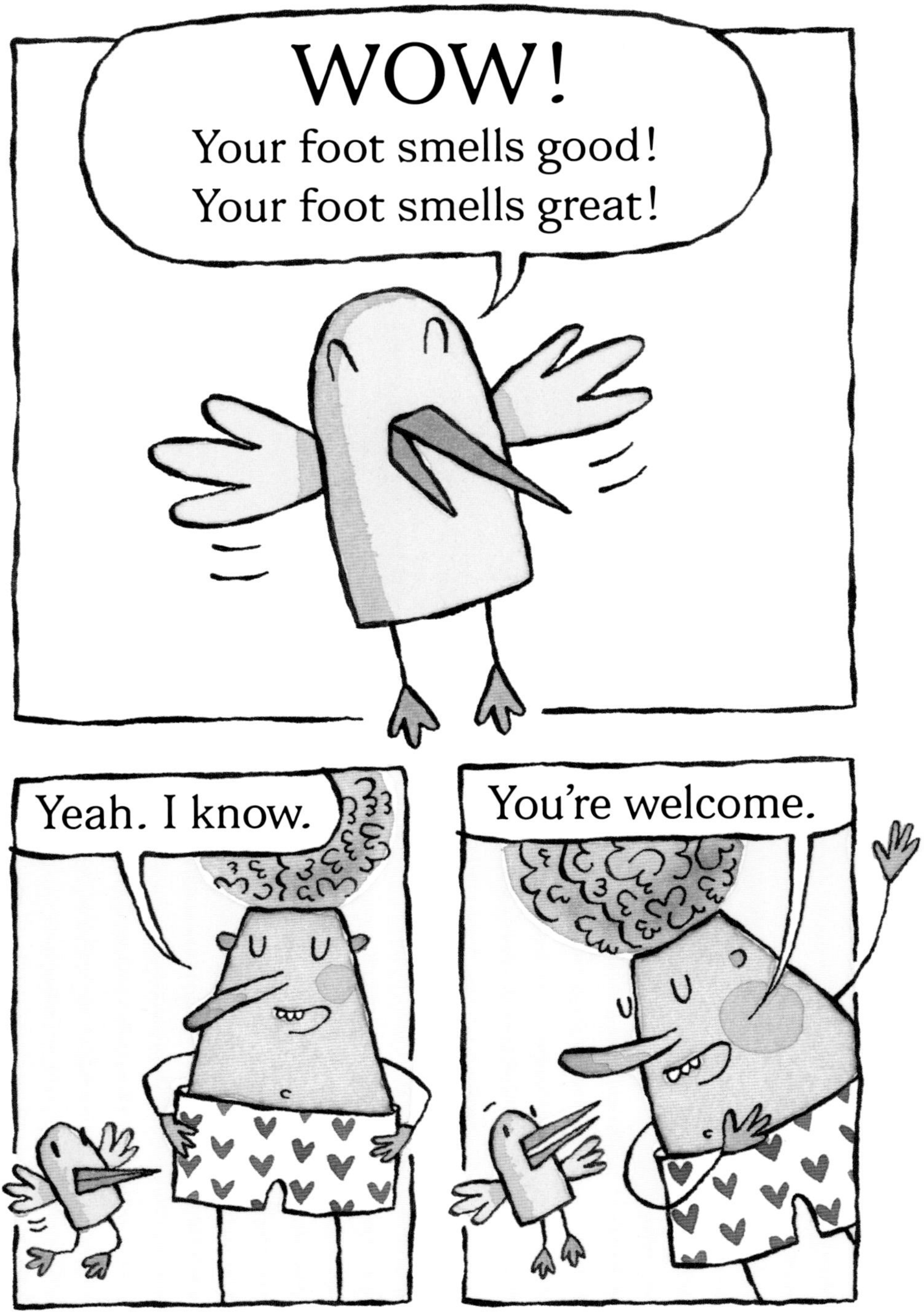
WOW!
Your foot smells good!
Your foot smells great!
Yeah. I know.
You're welcome.

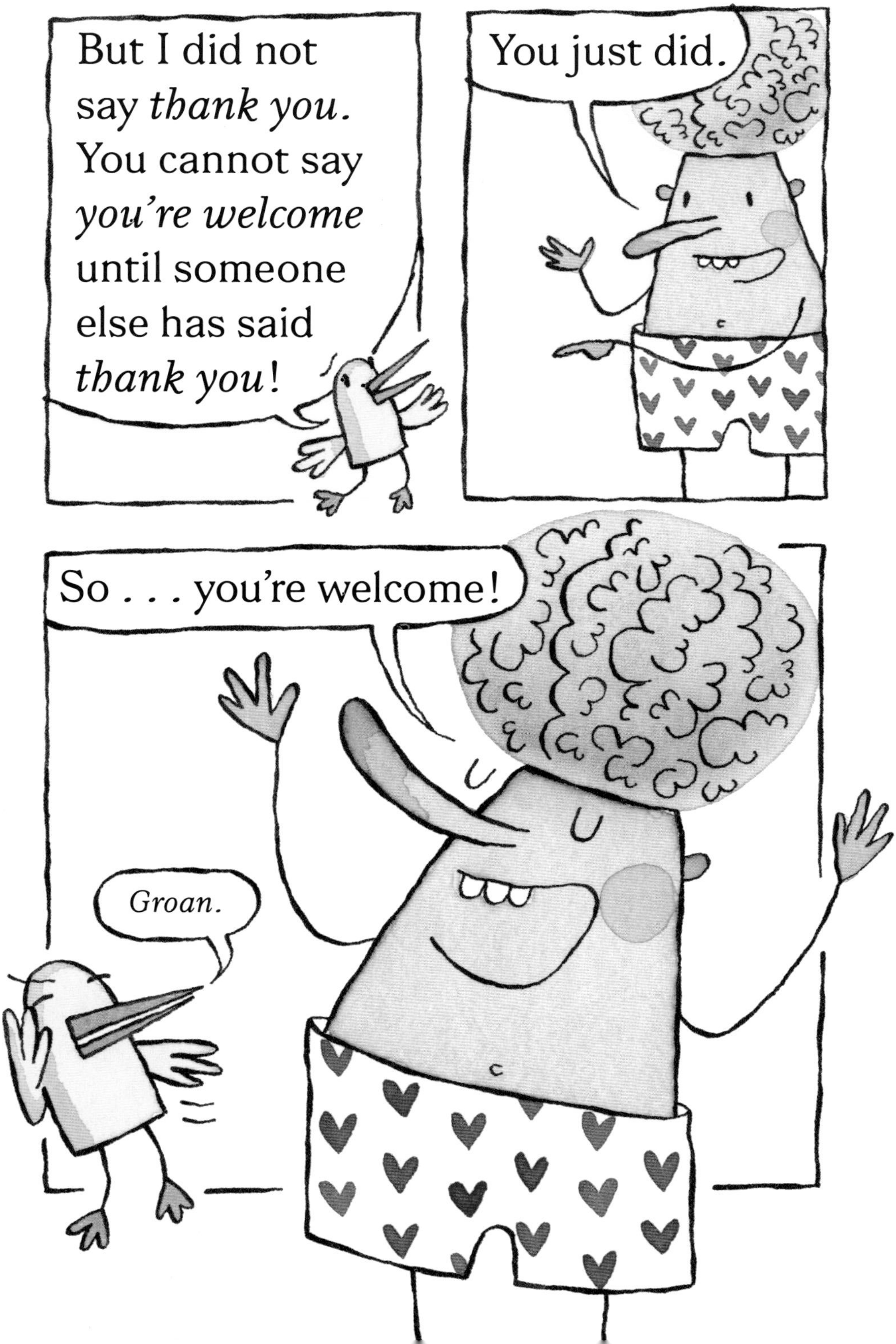

But I did not say *thank you.* You cannot say *you're welcome* until someone else has said *thank you*!
You just did.
So . . . you're welcome!
Groan.

Chapter 2

Spot

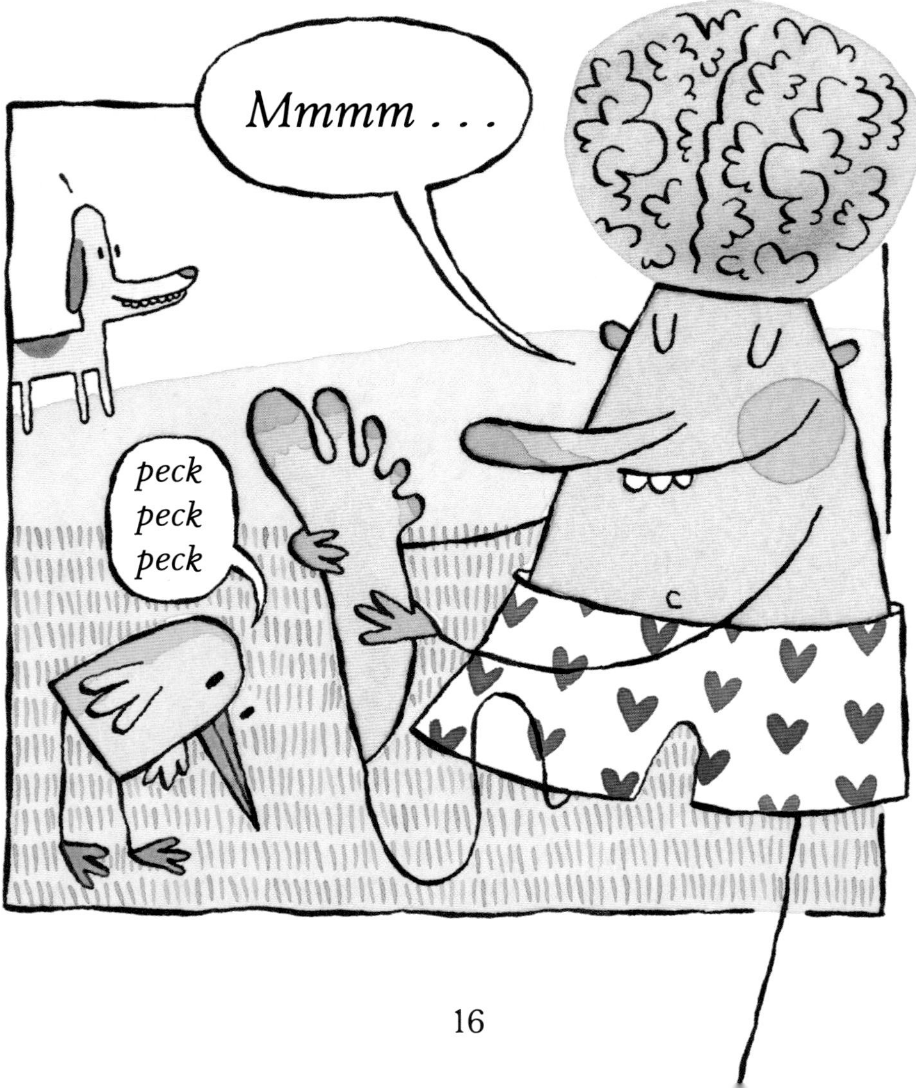
Mmmm . . .
peck
peck
peck

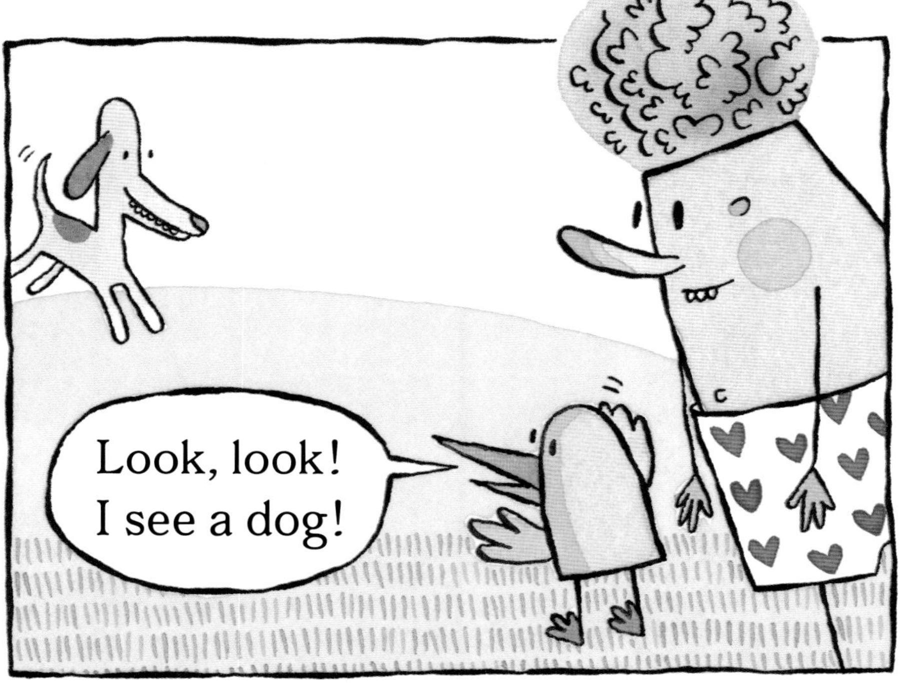
Look, look! I see a dog!

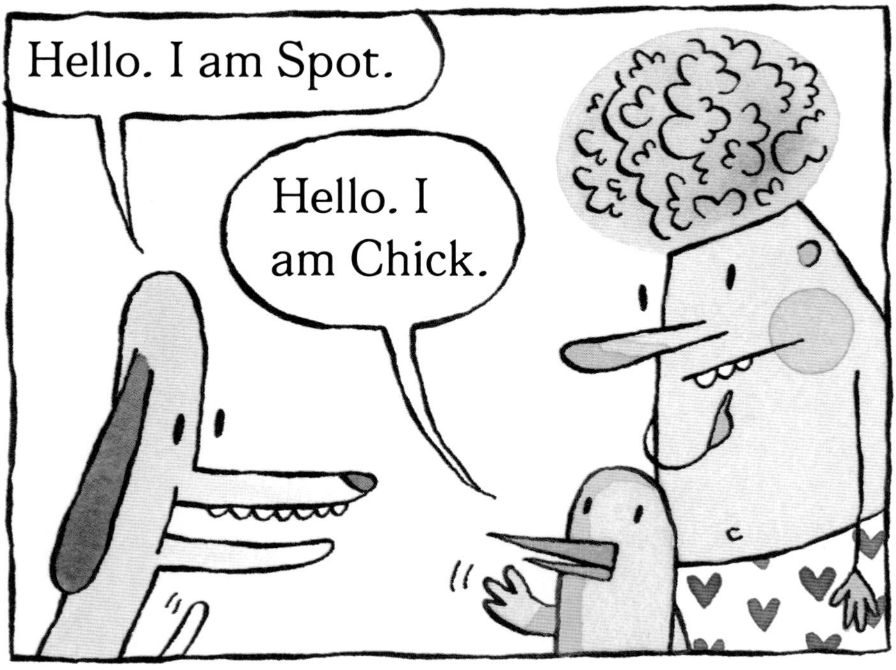
Hello. I am Spot.
Hello. I am Chick.

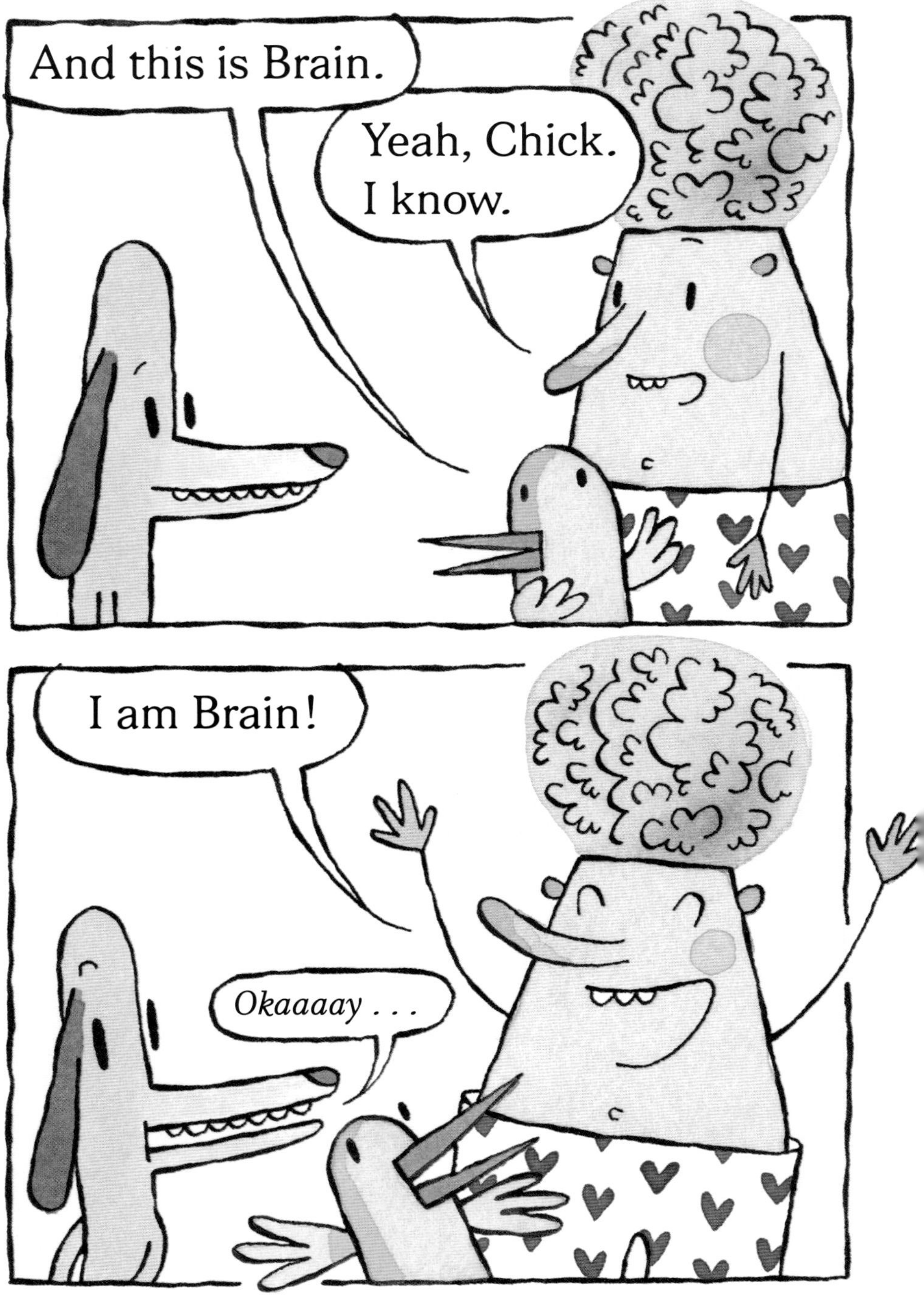
And this is Brain.
Yeah, Chick. I know.
I am Brain!
Okaaaay . . .

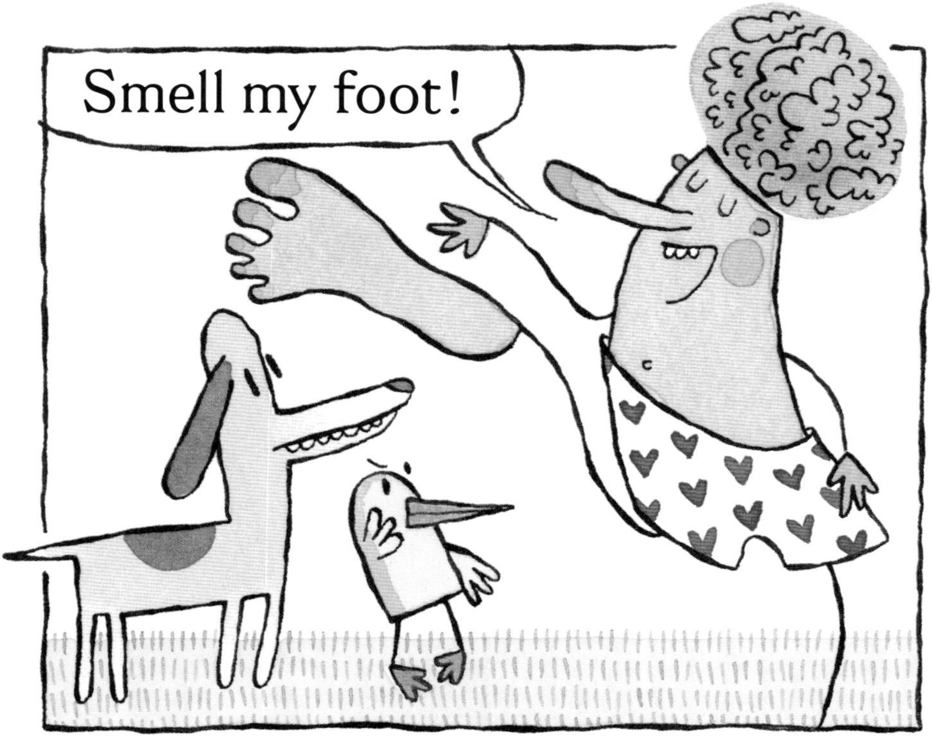
Smell my foot!

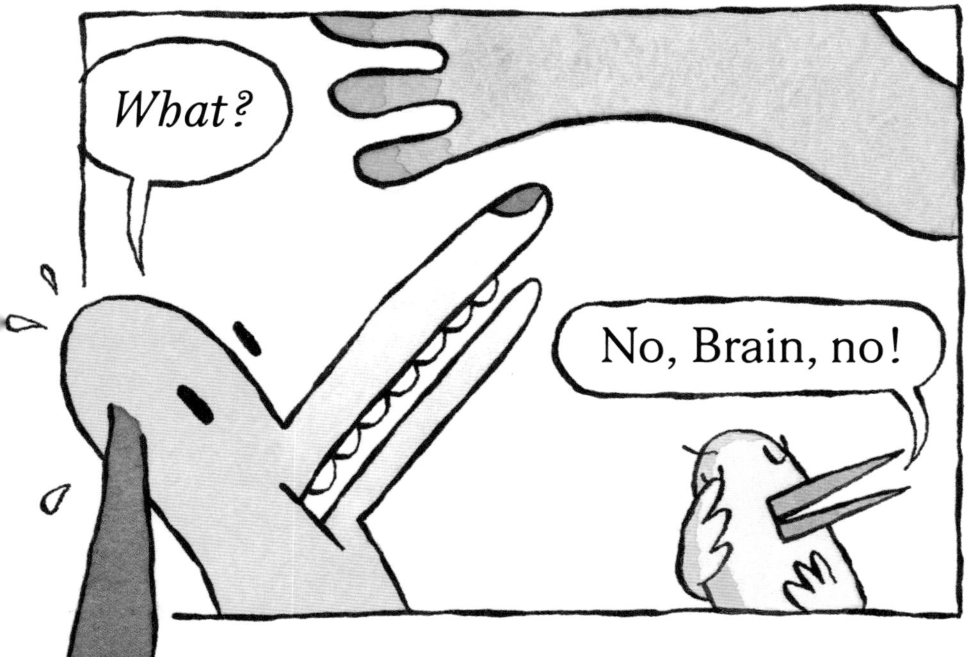
What?
No, Brain, no!

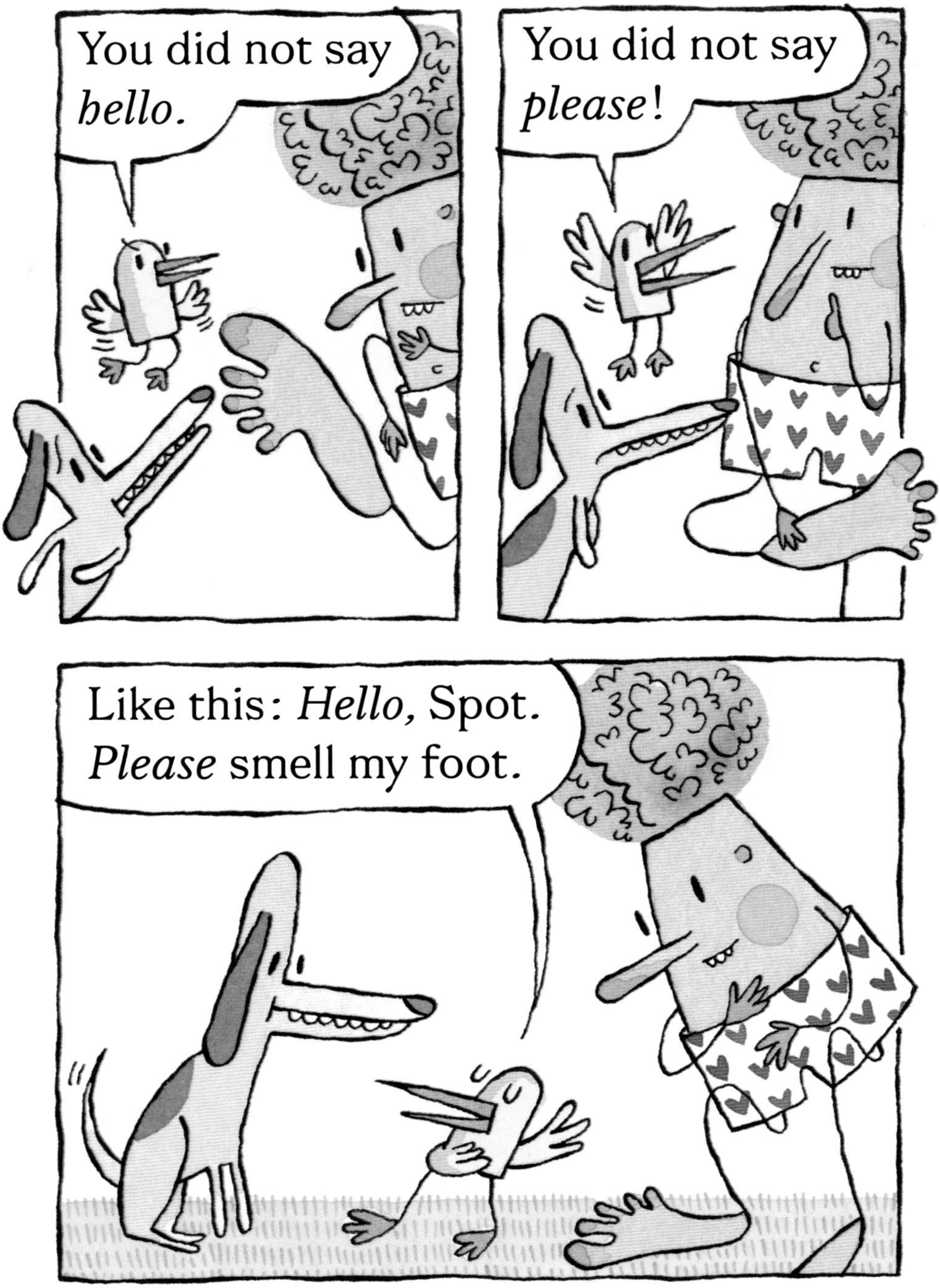
You did not say *hello*.
You did not say *please*!
Like this: *Hello*, Spot. *Please* smell my foot.

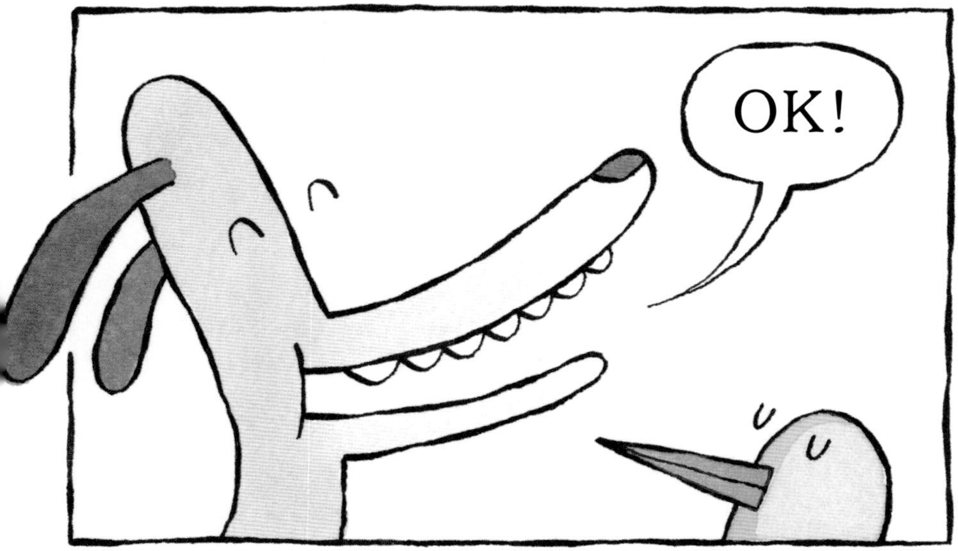
OK!

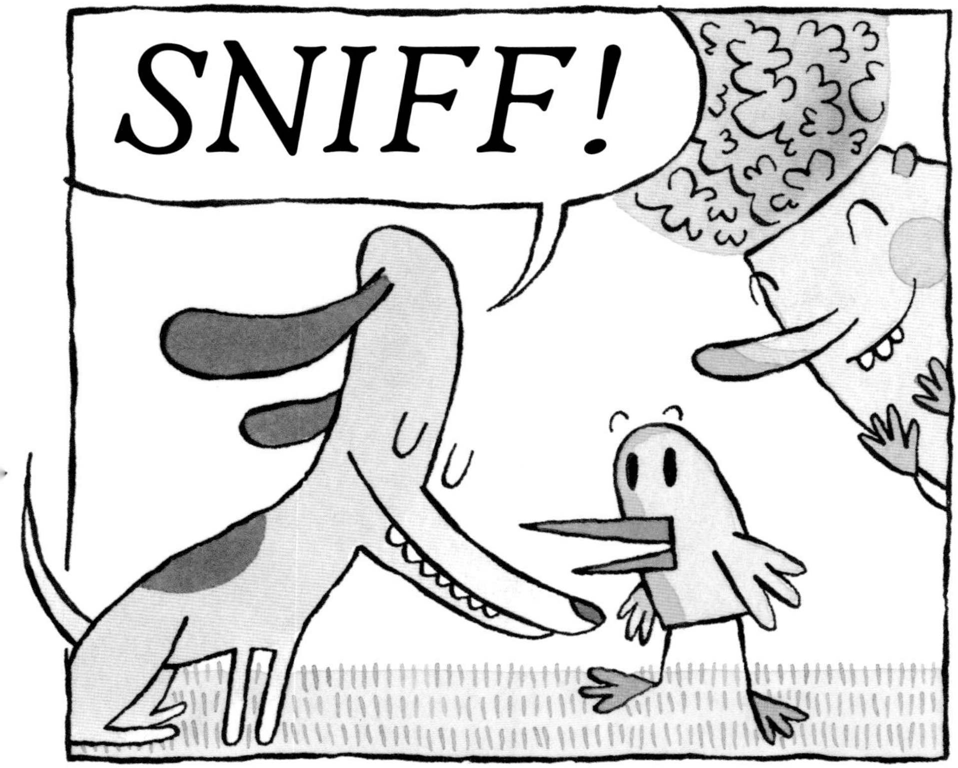
SNIFF!

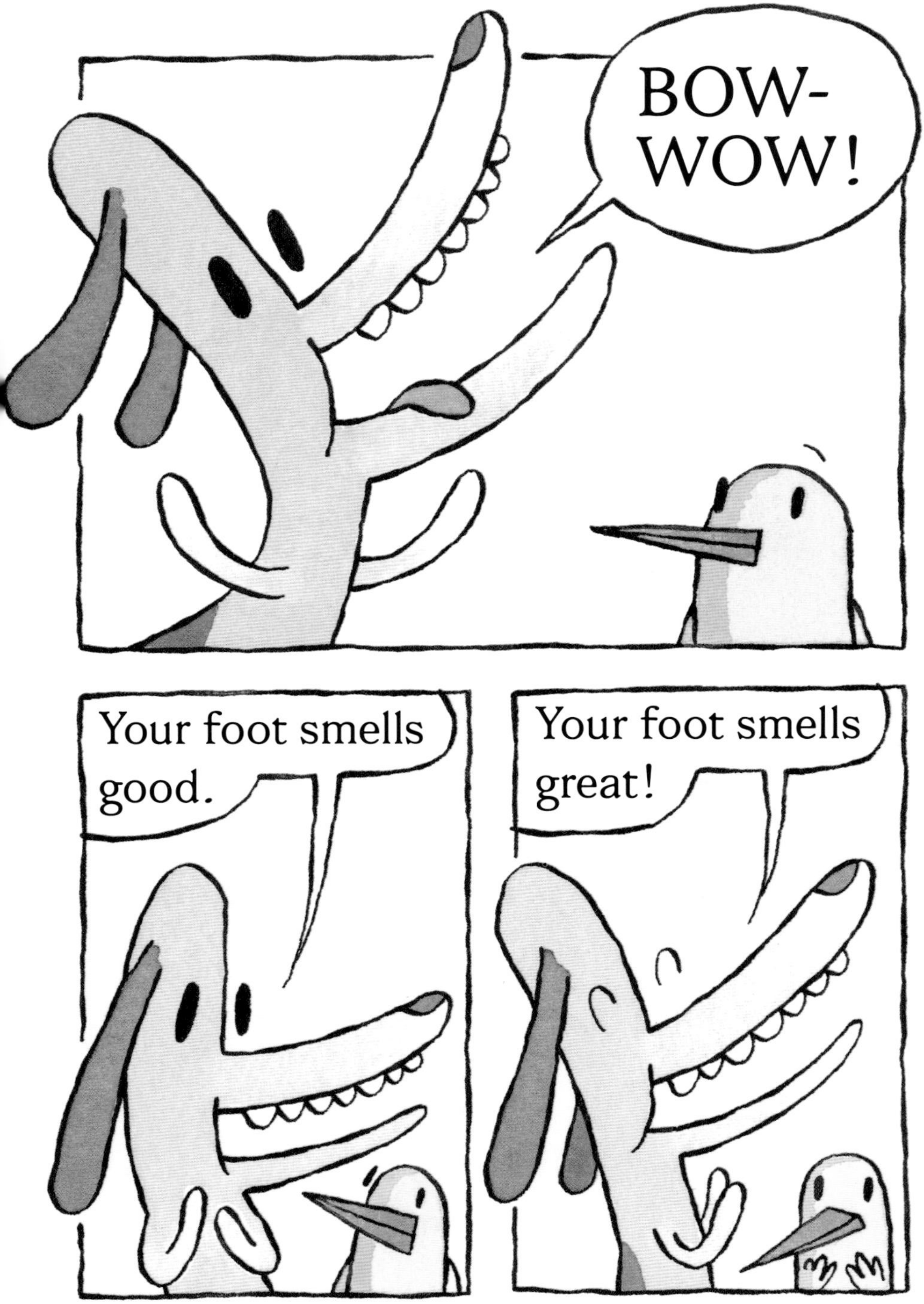
BOW-WOW!
Your foot smells good.
Your foot smells great!

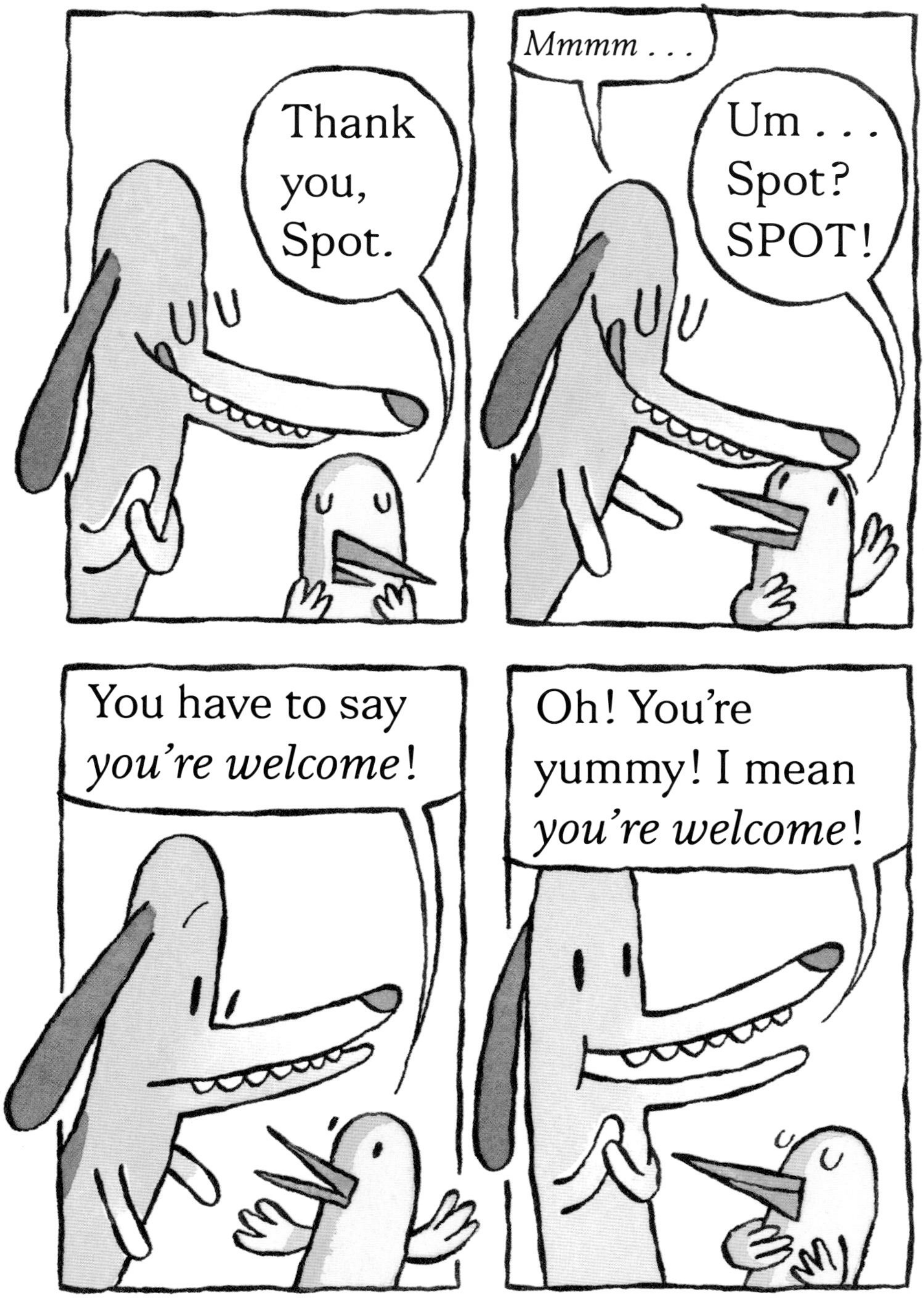

Thank you, Spot.
Mmmm . . .
Um . . . Spot? SPOT!
You have to say *you're welcome*!
Oh! You're yummy! I mean *you're welcome*!

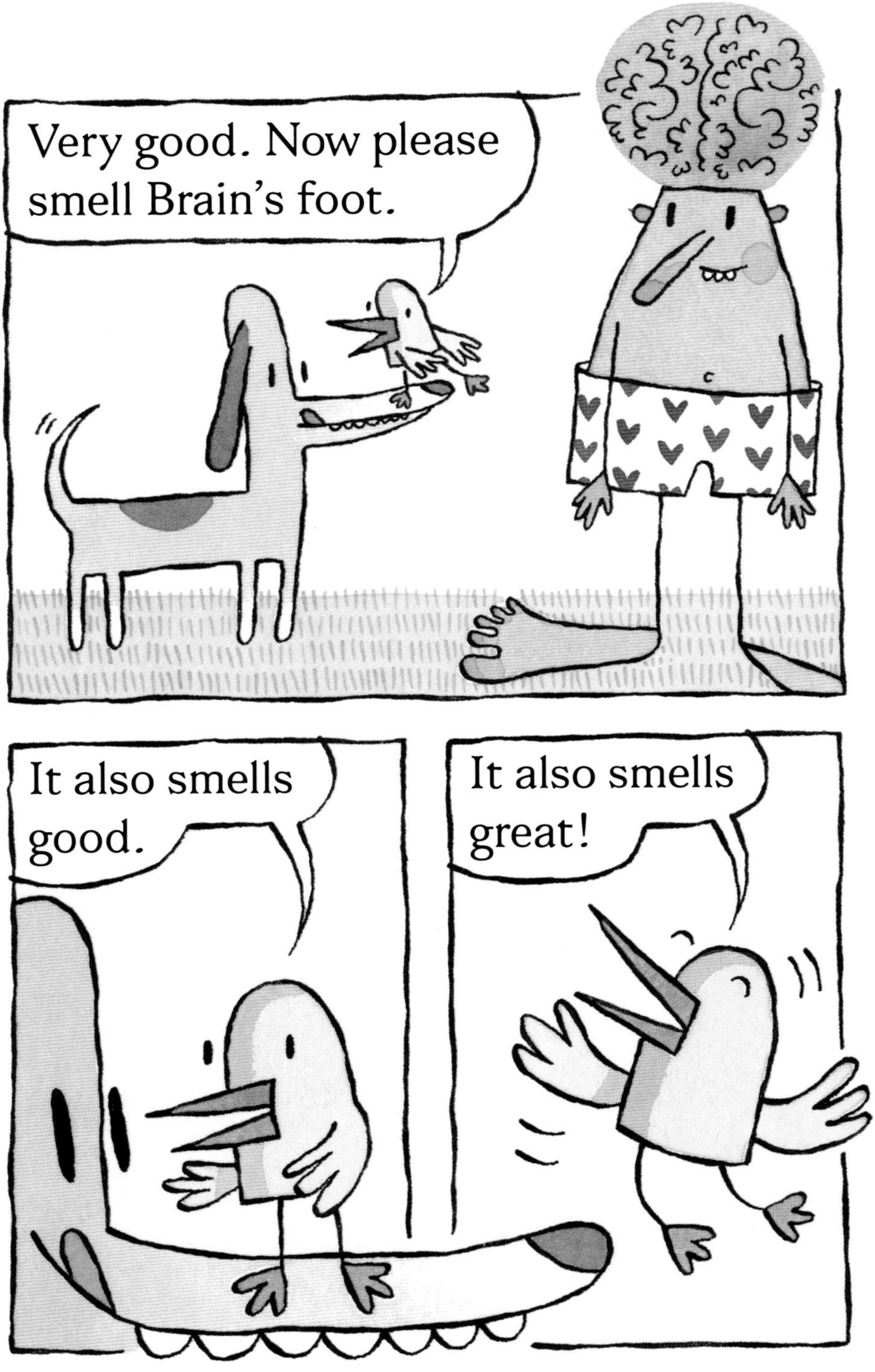
Very good. Now please smell Brain's foot.
It also smells good.
It also smells great!

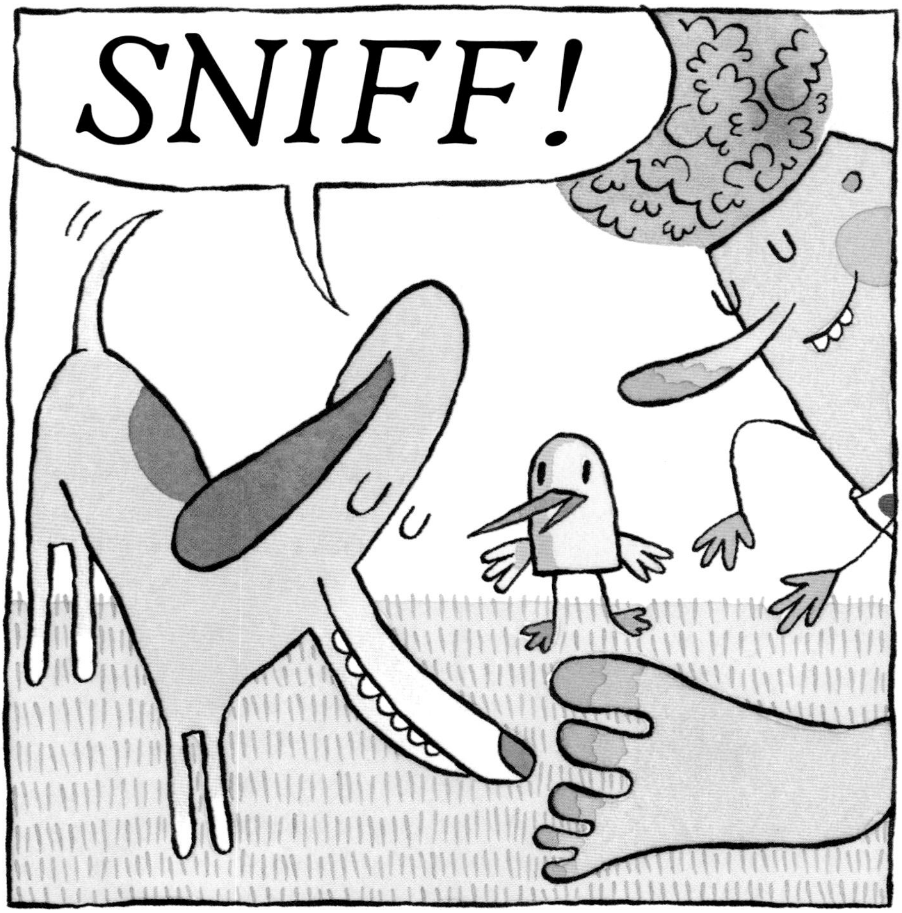
SNIFF!

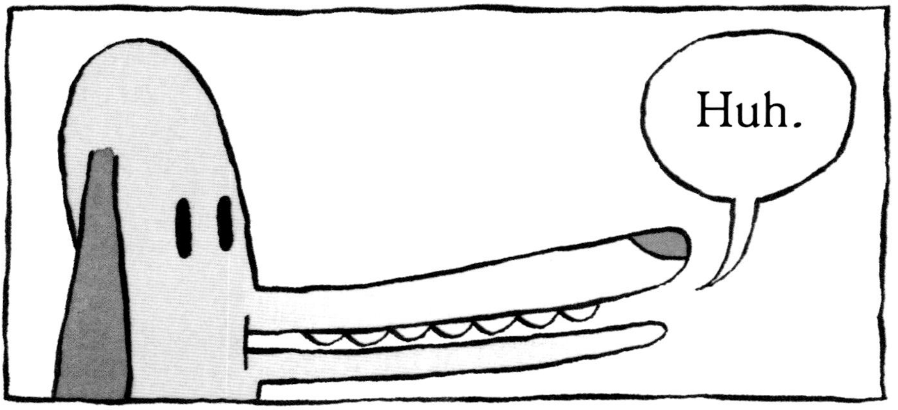
Huh.

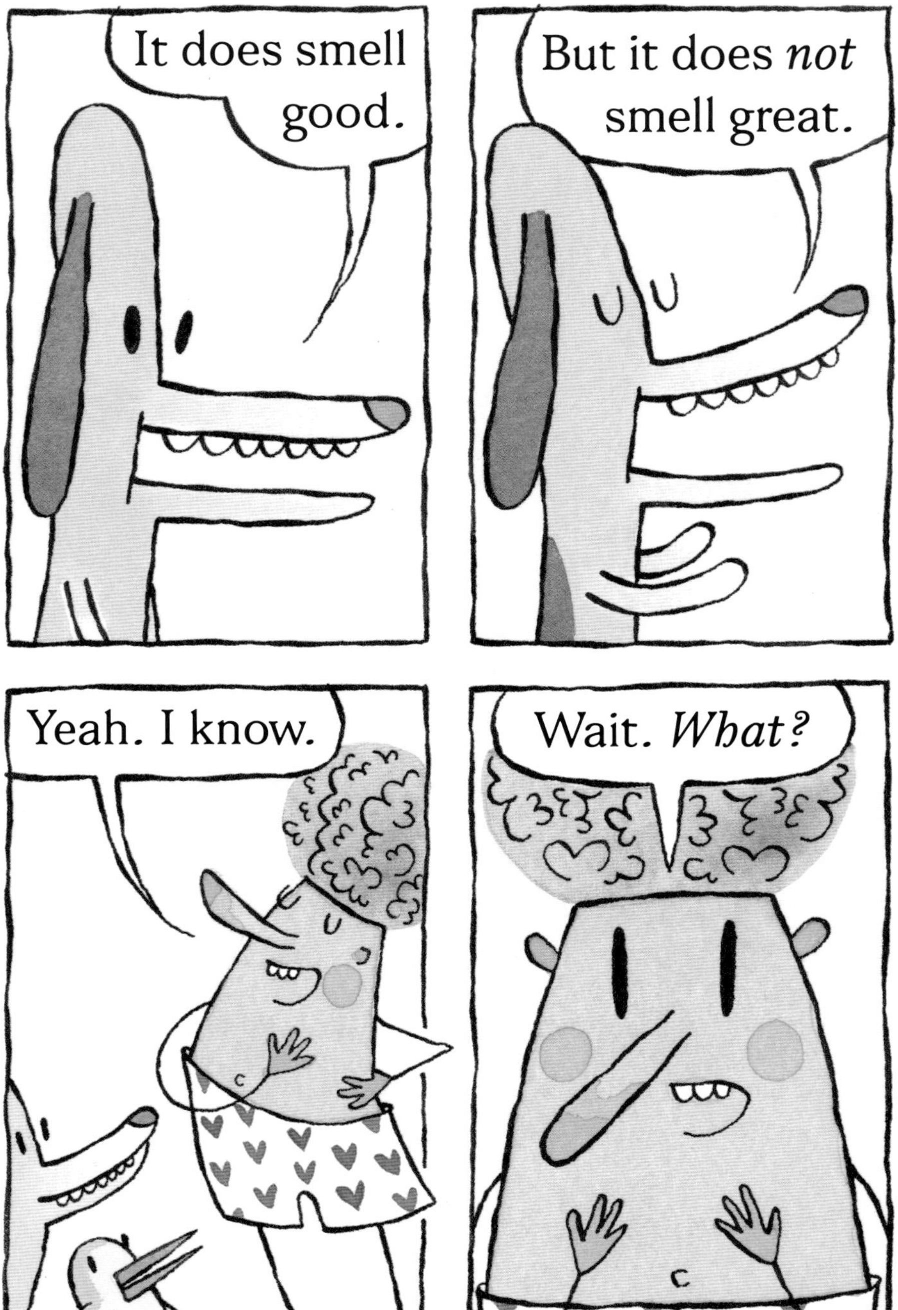
It does smell good.
But it does *not* smell great.
Yeah. I know.
Wait. *What?*

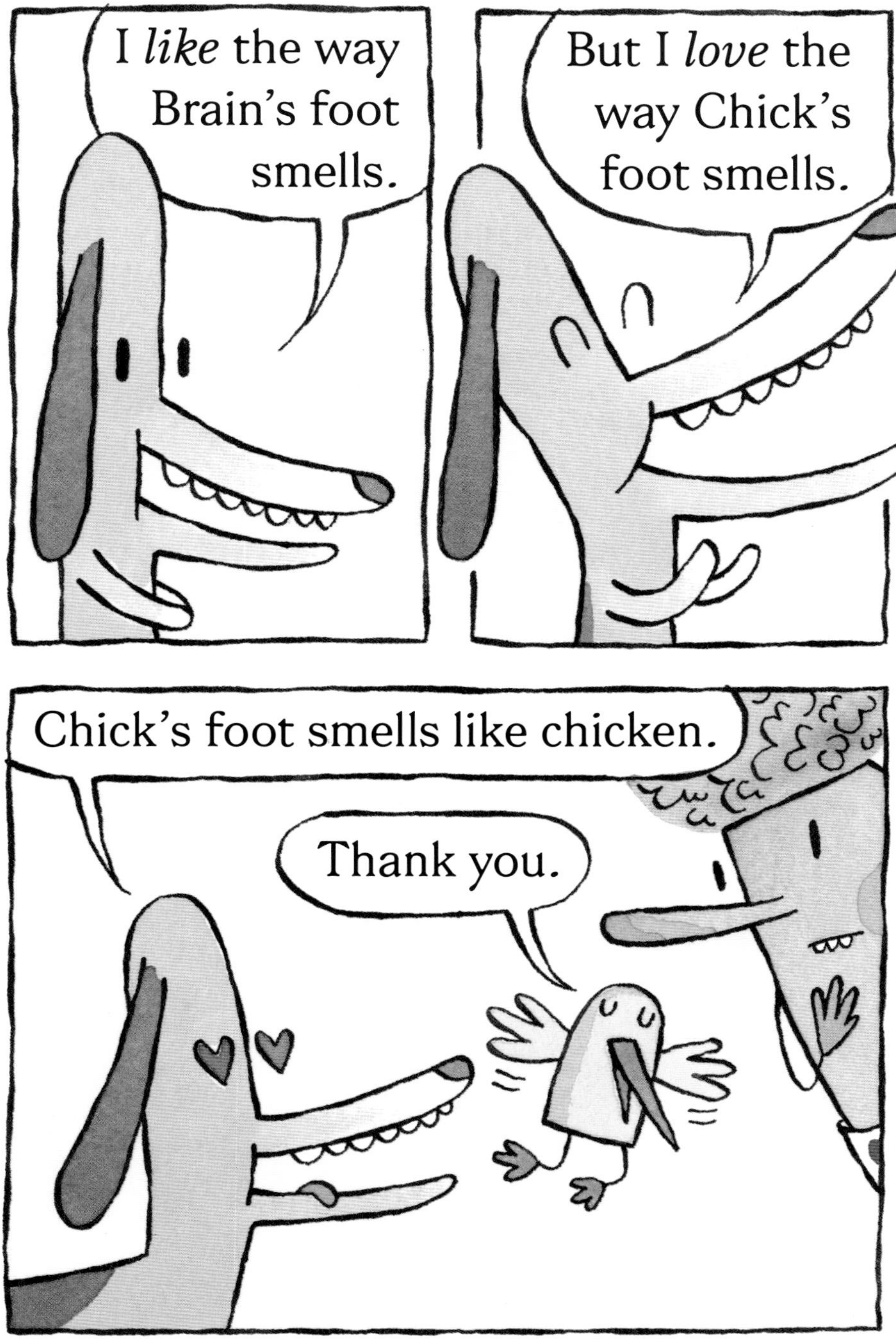
I *like* the way Brain's foot smells.
But I *love* the way Chick's foot smells.
Chick's foot smells like chicken.
Thank you.

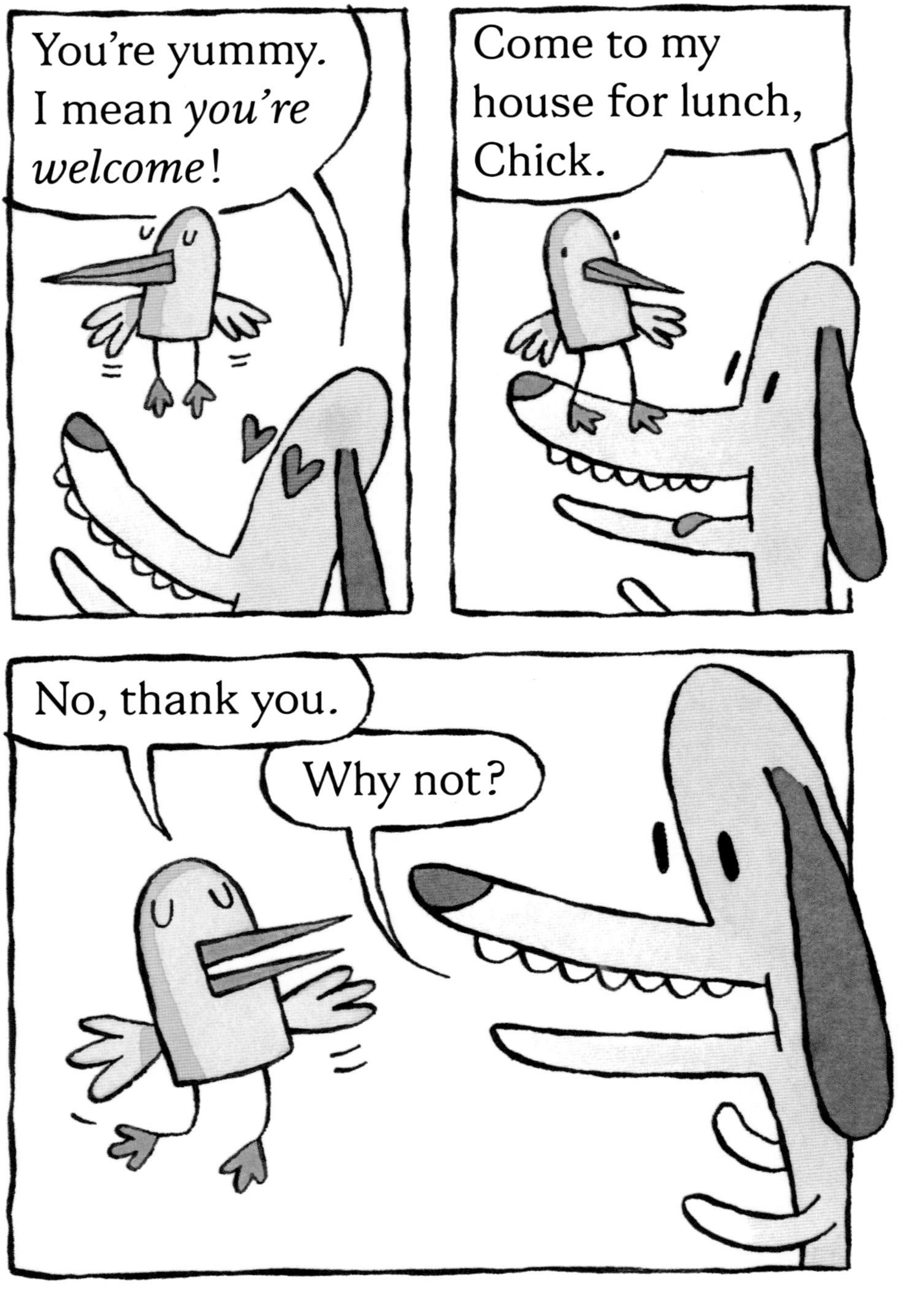
You're yummy.
I mean *you're welcome*!
Come to my house for lunch, Chick.
No, thank you.
Why not?

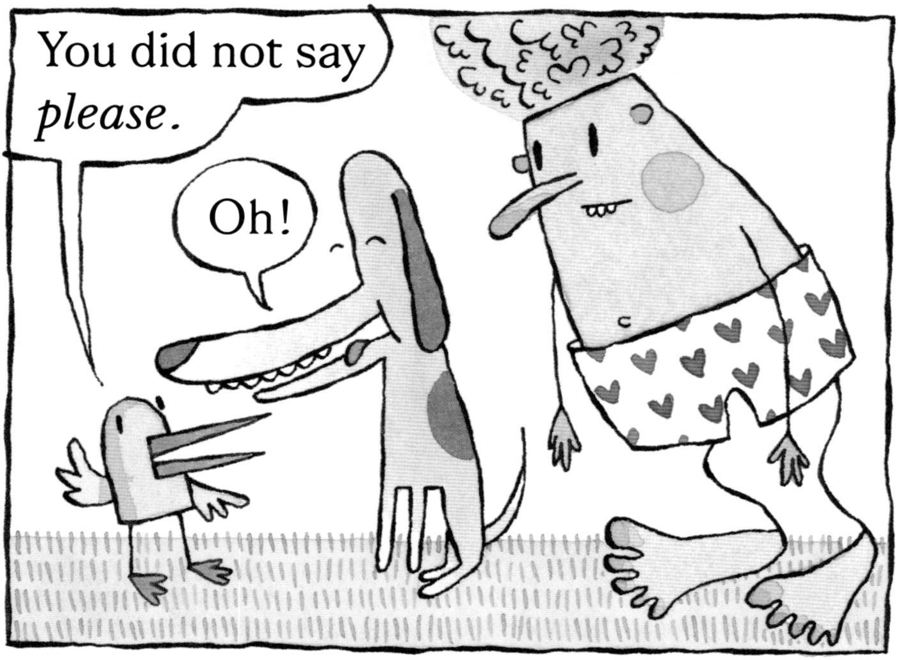
You did not say *please*.
Oh!

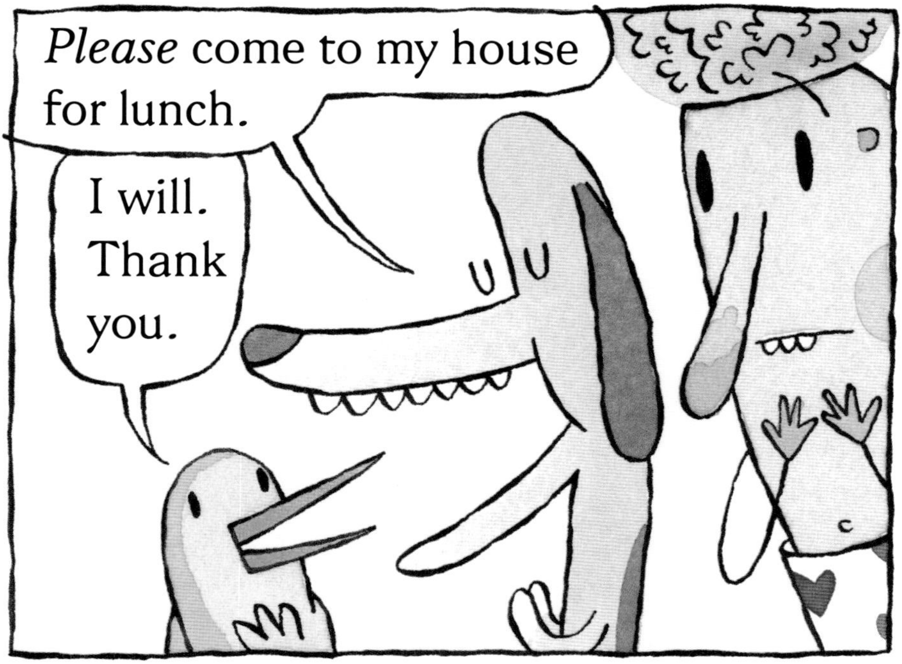
Please come to my house for lunch.
I will. Thank you.

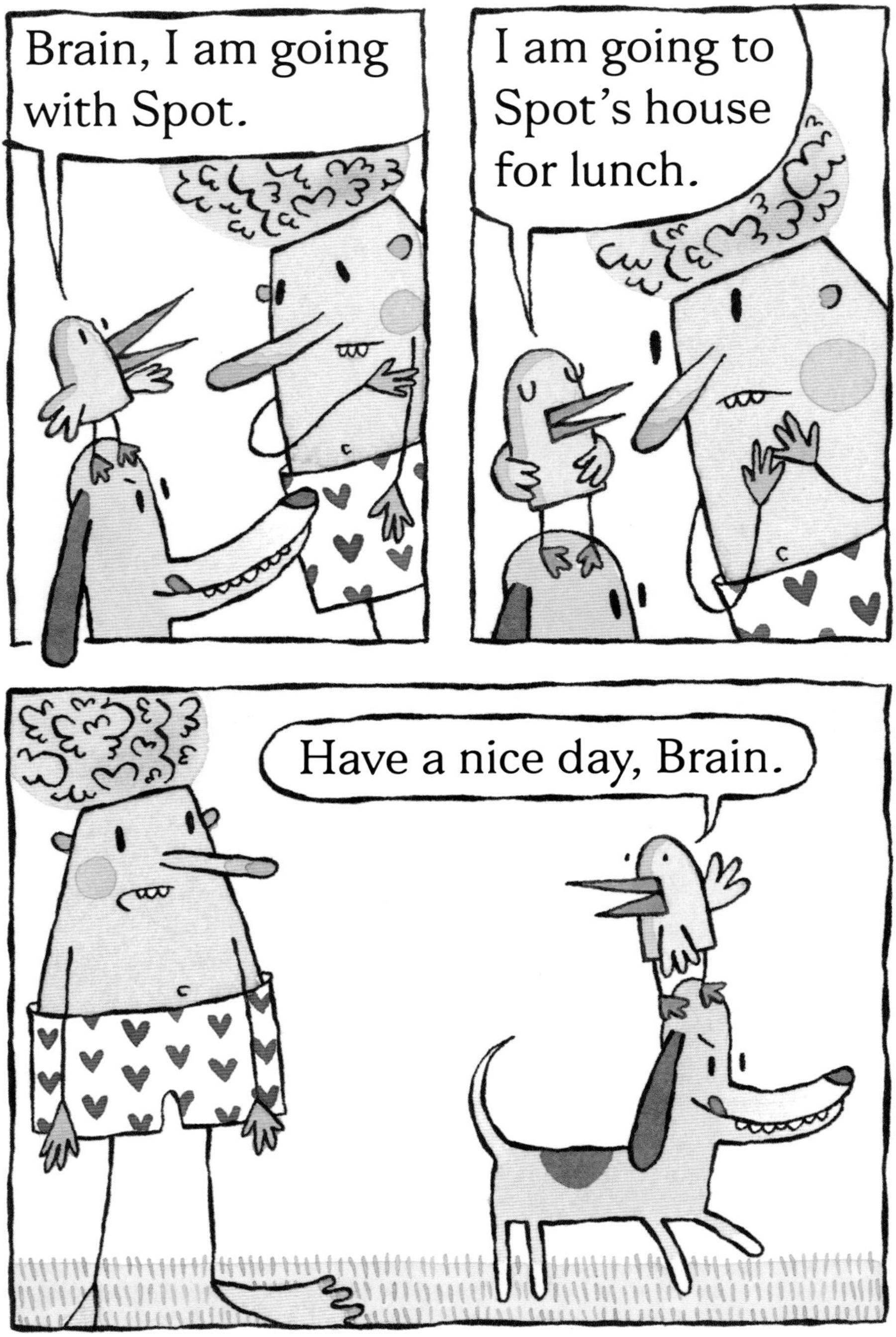
Brain, I am going with Spot.
I am going to Spot's house for lunch.
Have a nice day, Brain.

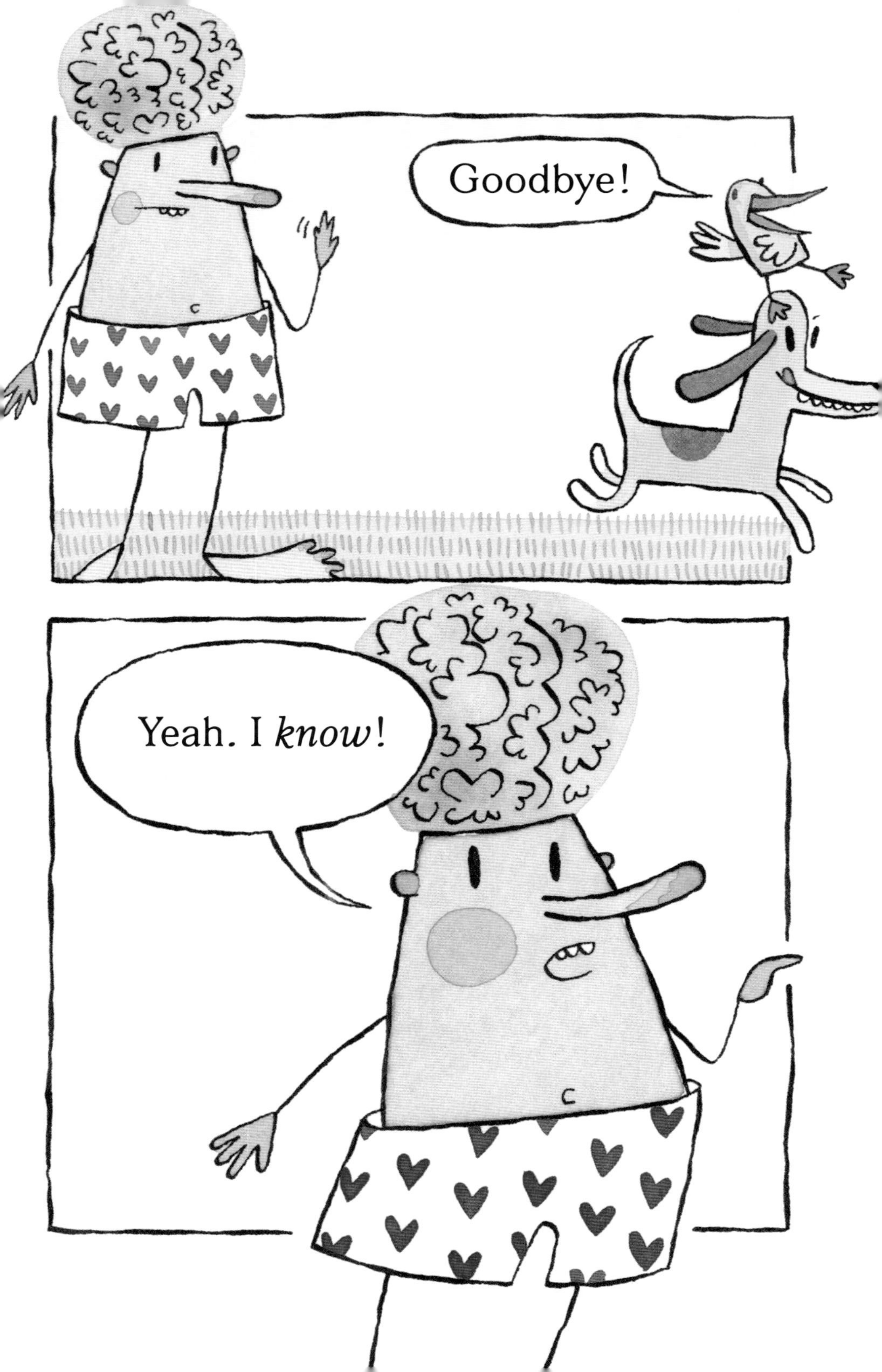
Goodbye!
Yeah. I *know*!

Chapter 3

Lunch

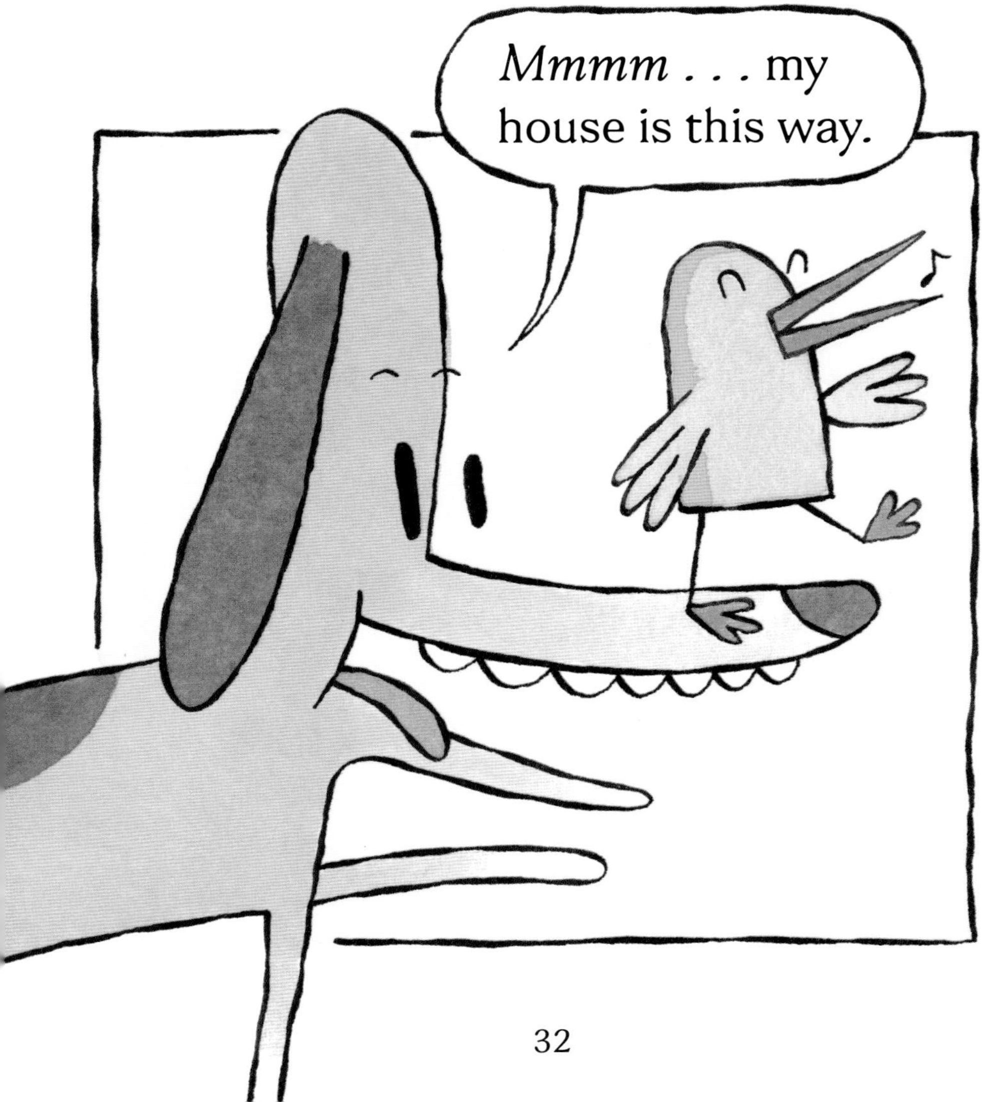
Mmmm . . . my house is this way.

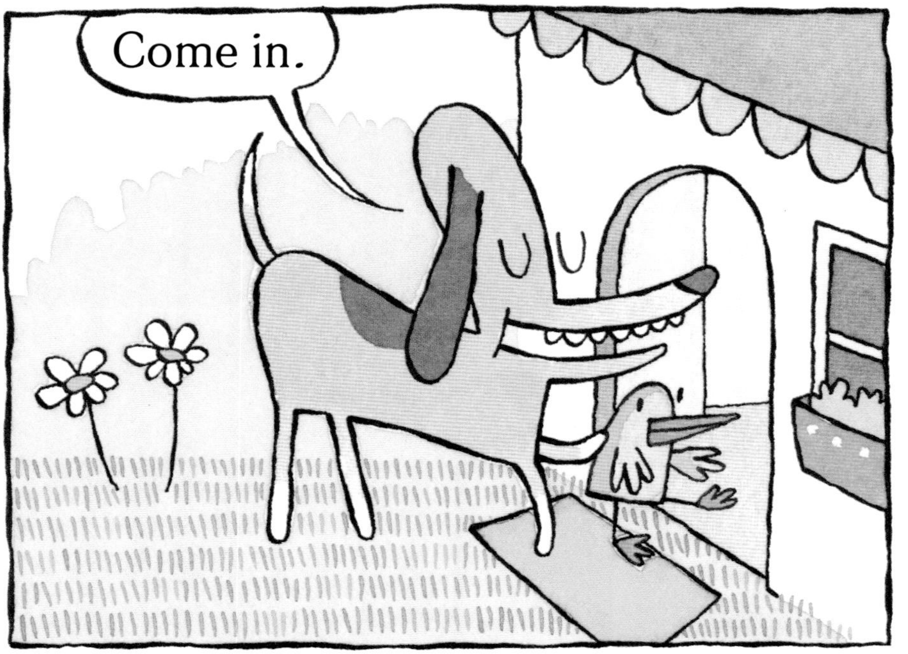
Come in.

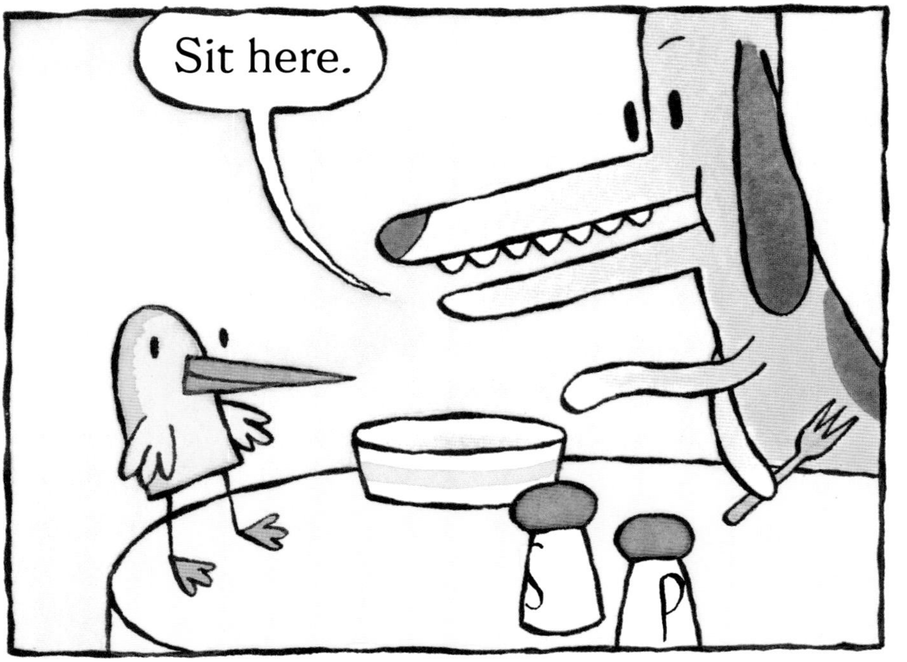
Sit here.
S
P

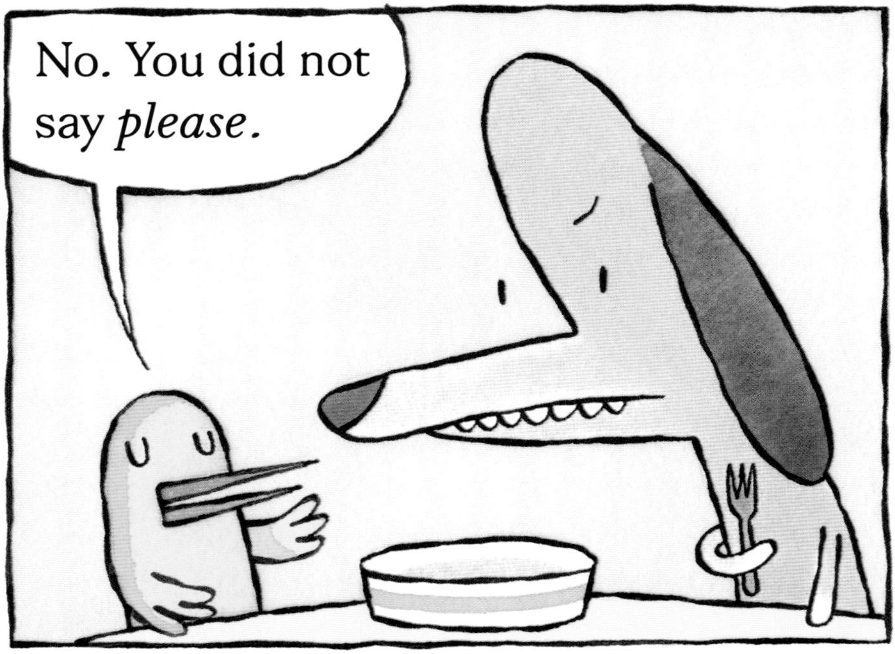
No. You did not say *please*.

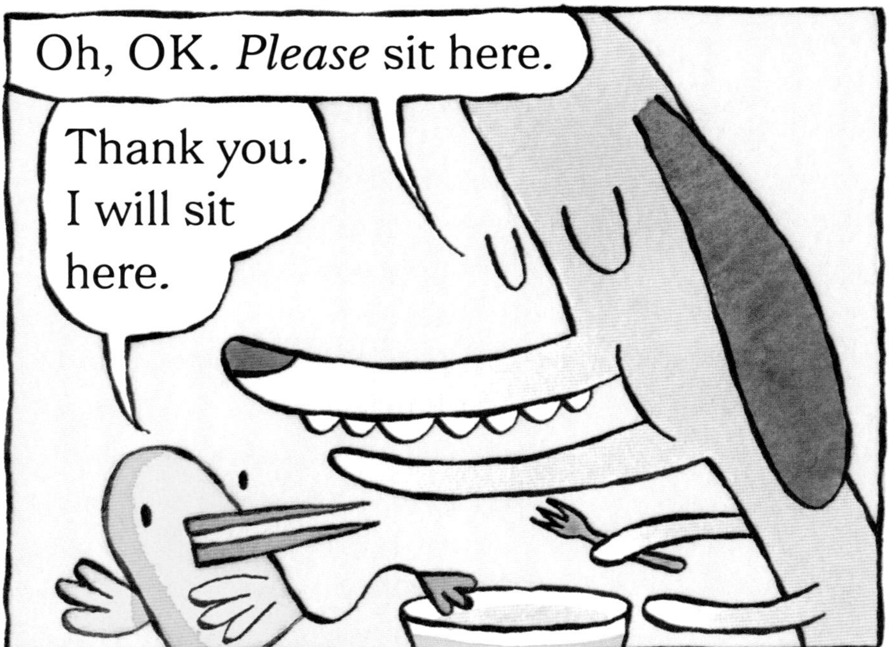
Oh, OK. *Please* sit here.
Thank you. I will sit here.

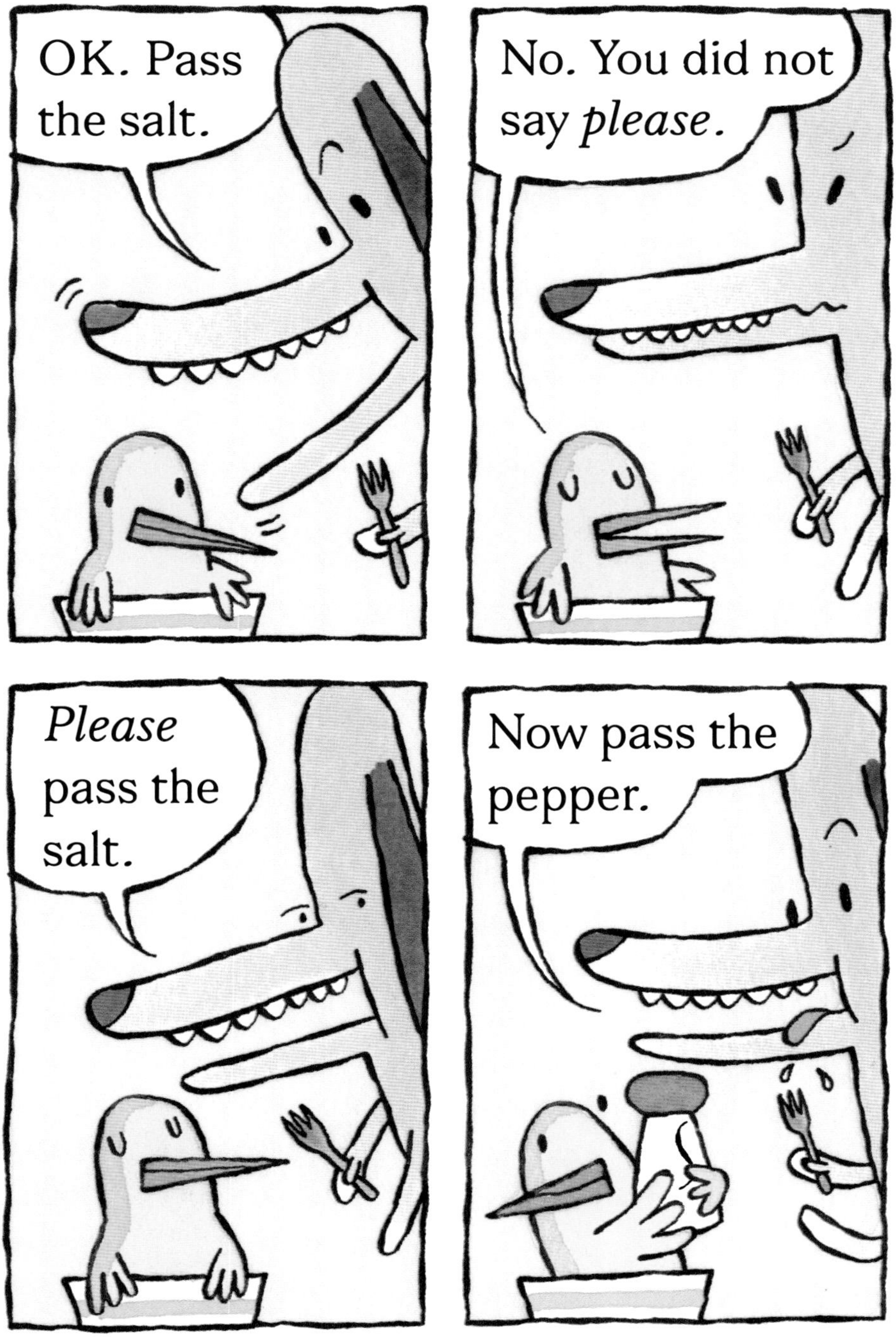
OK. Pass the salt.
No. You did not say *please*.
Please pass the salt.
Now pass the pepper.

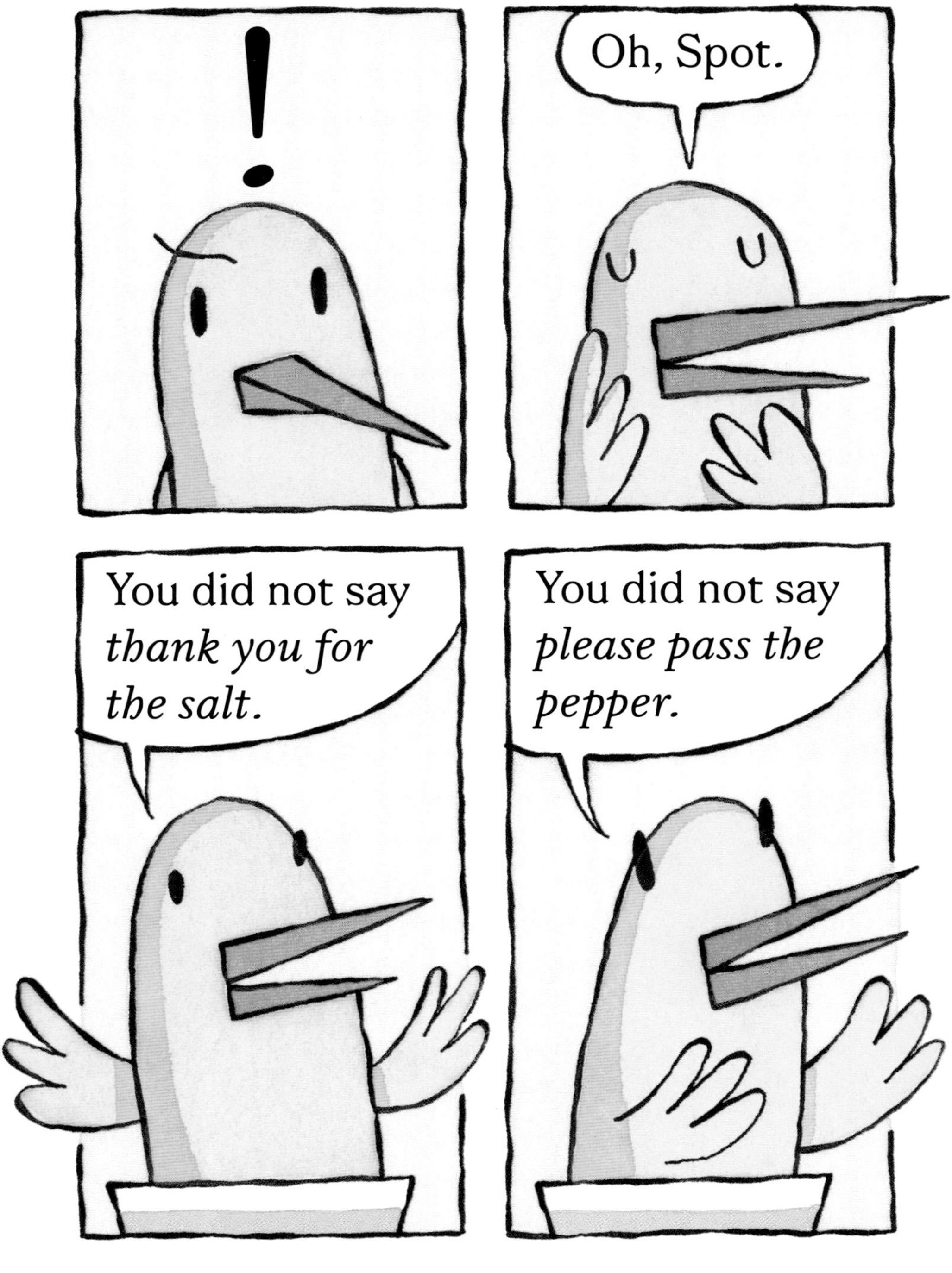
!
Oh, Spot.
You did not say *thank you for the salt.*
You did not say *please pass the pepper.*

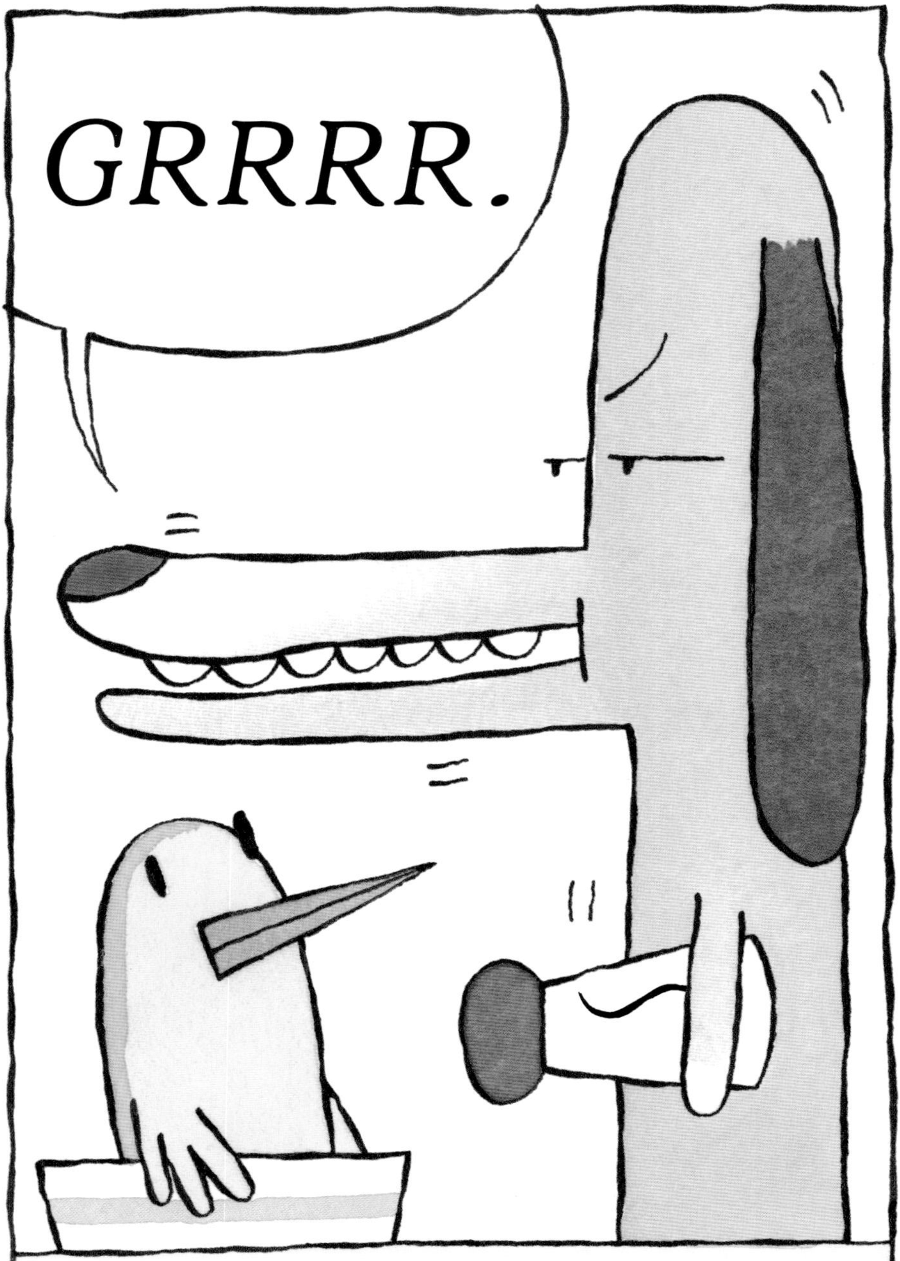
GRRRR.

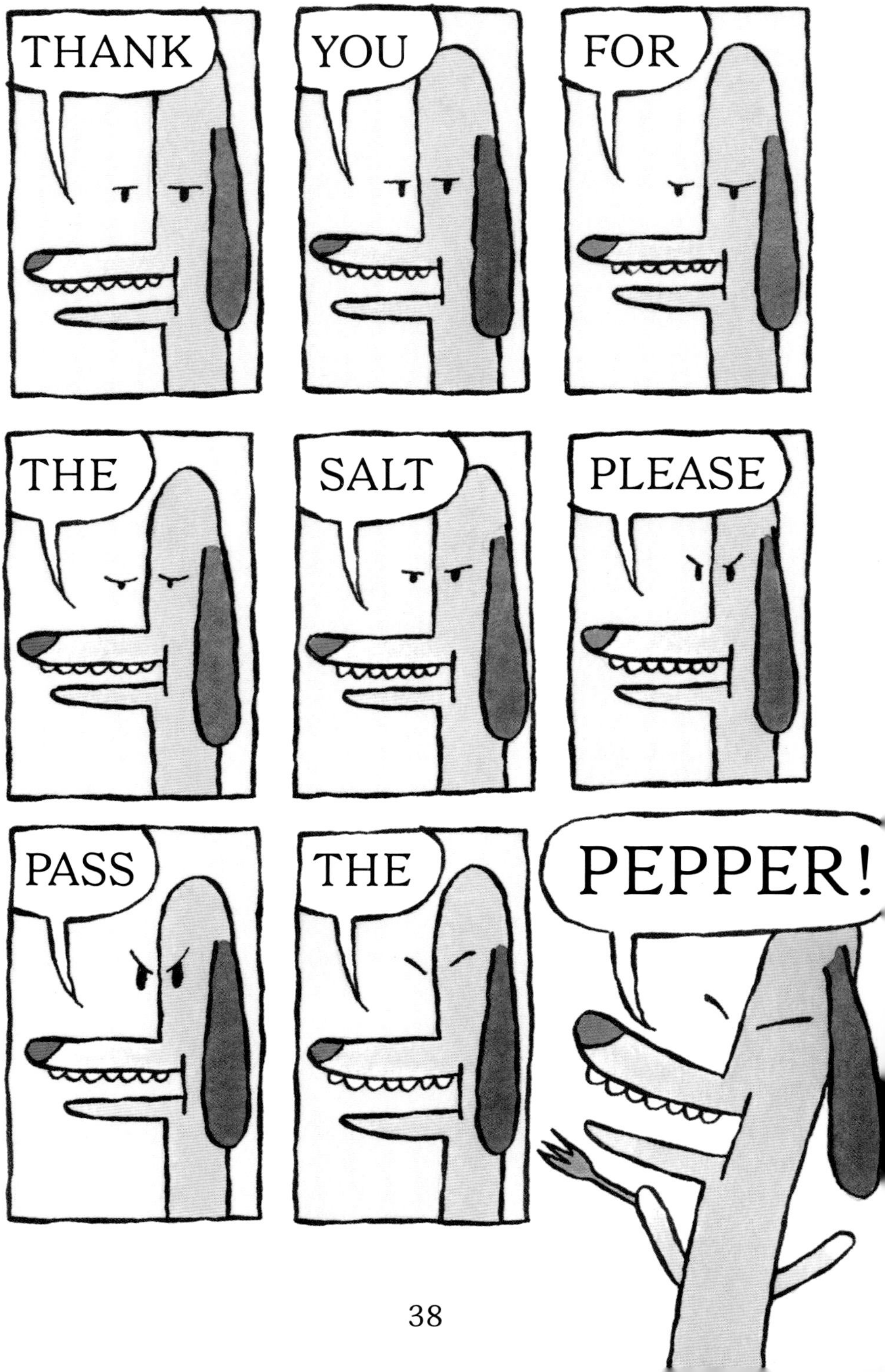
THANK
YOU
FOR
THE
SALT
PLEASE
PASS
THE
PEPPER!

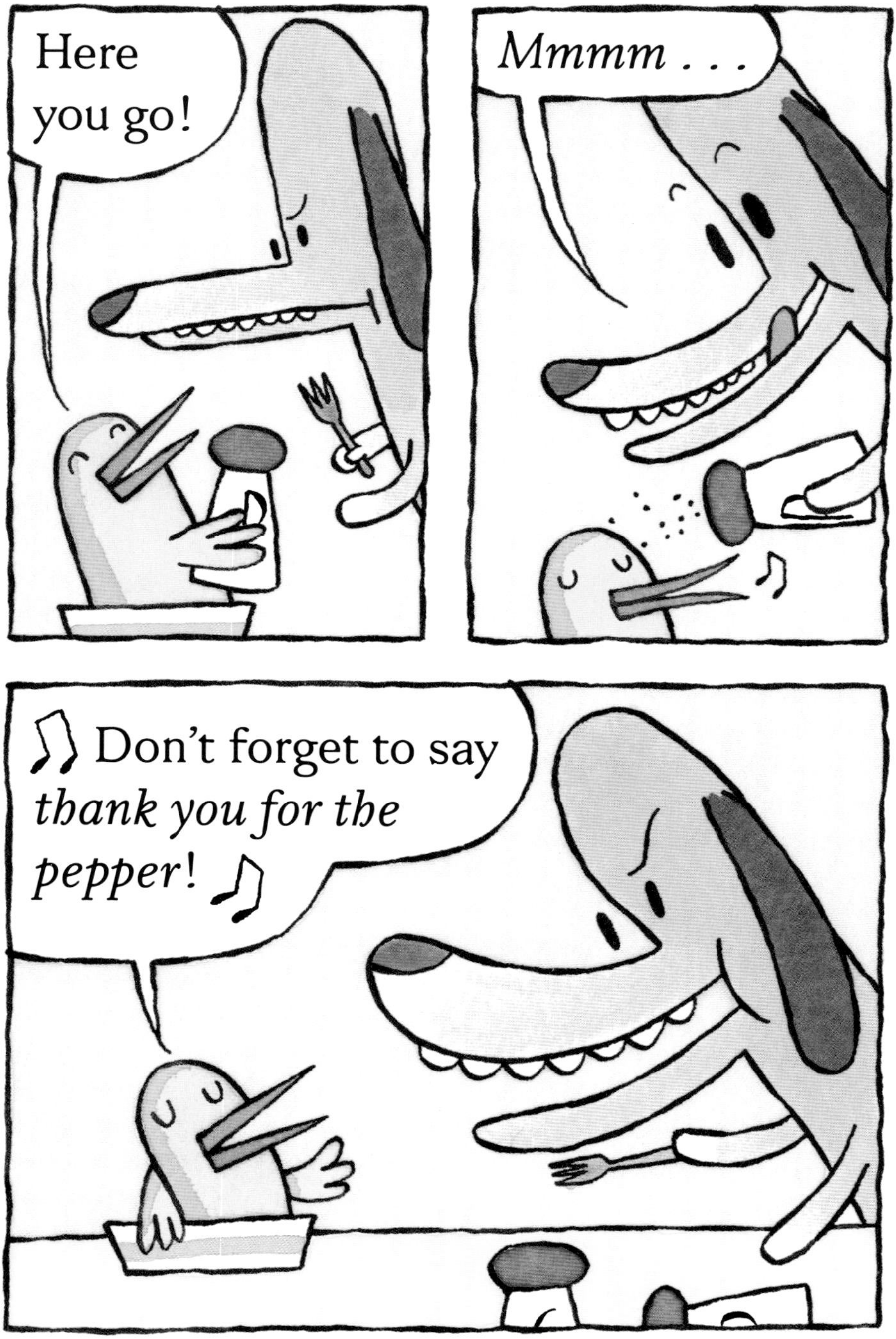
Here you go!
Mmmm . . .
♫ Don't forget to say *thank you for the pepper!* ♫

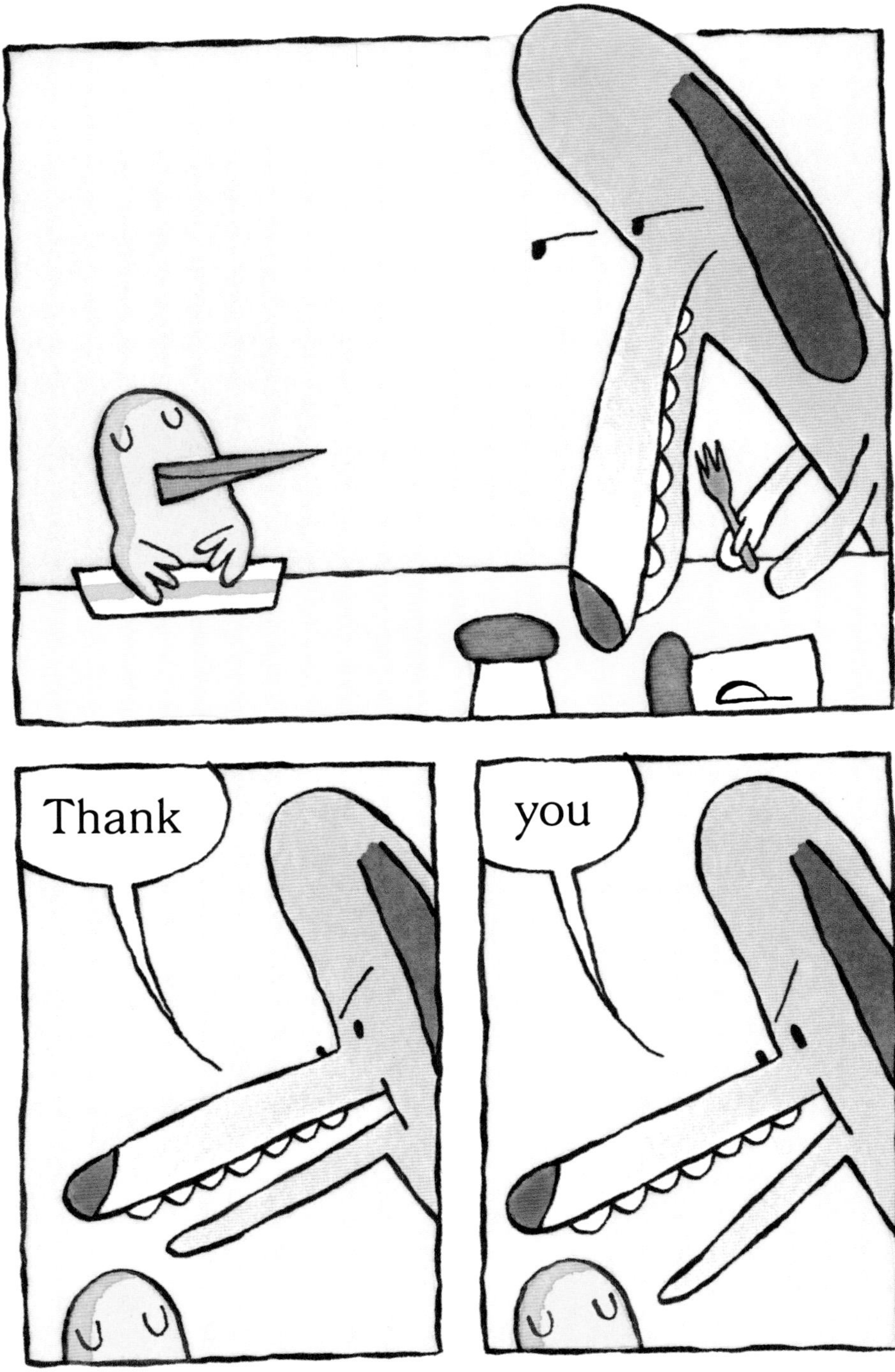
Thank
you

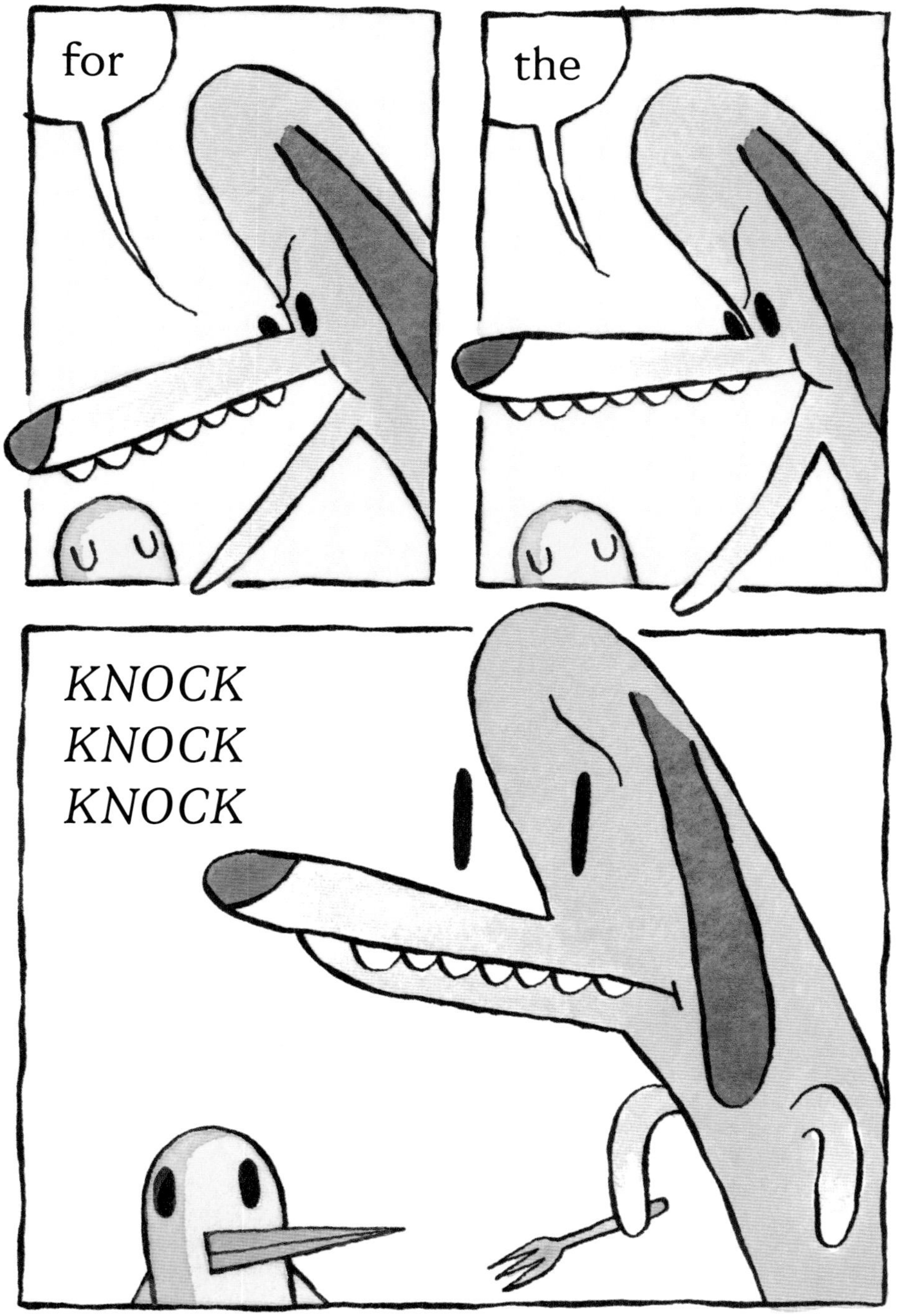
for
the
KNOCK
KNOCK
KNOCK

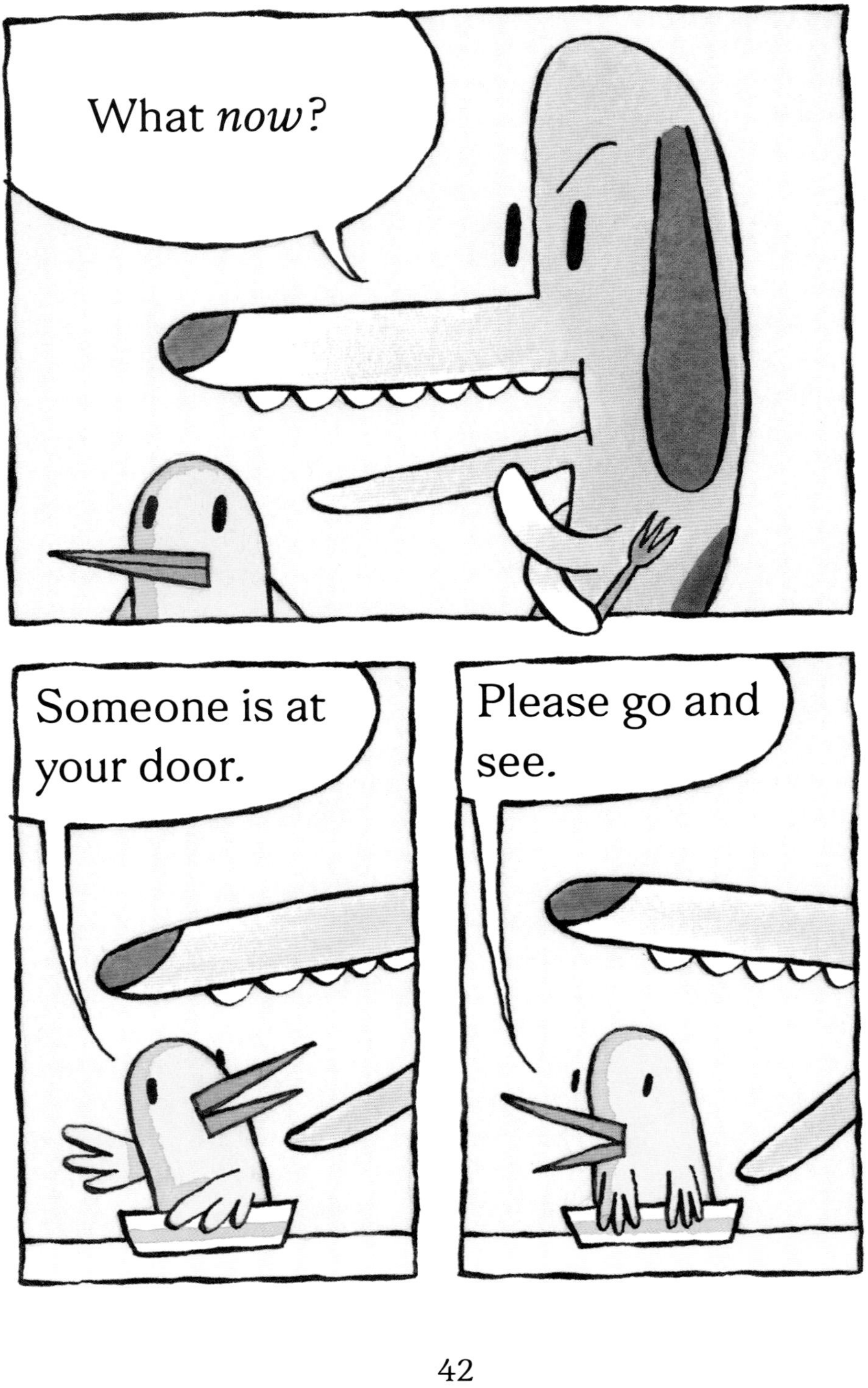
What *now*?
Someone is at your door.
Please go and see.

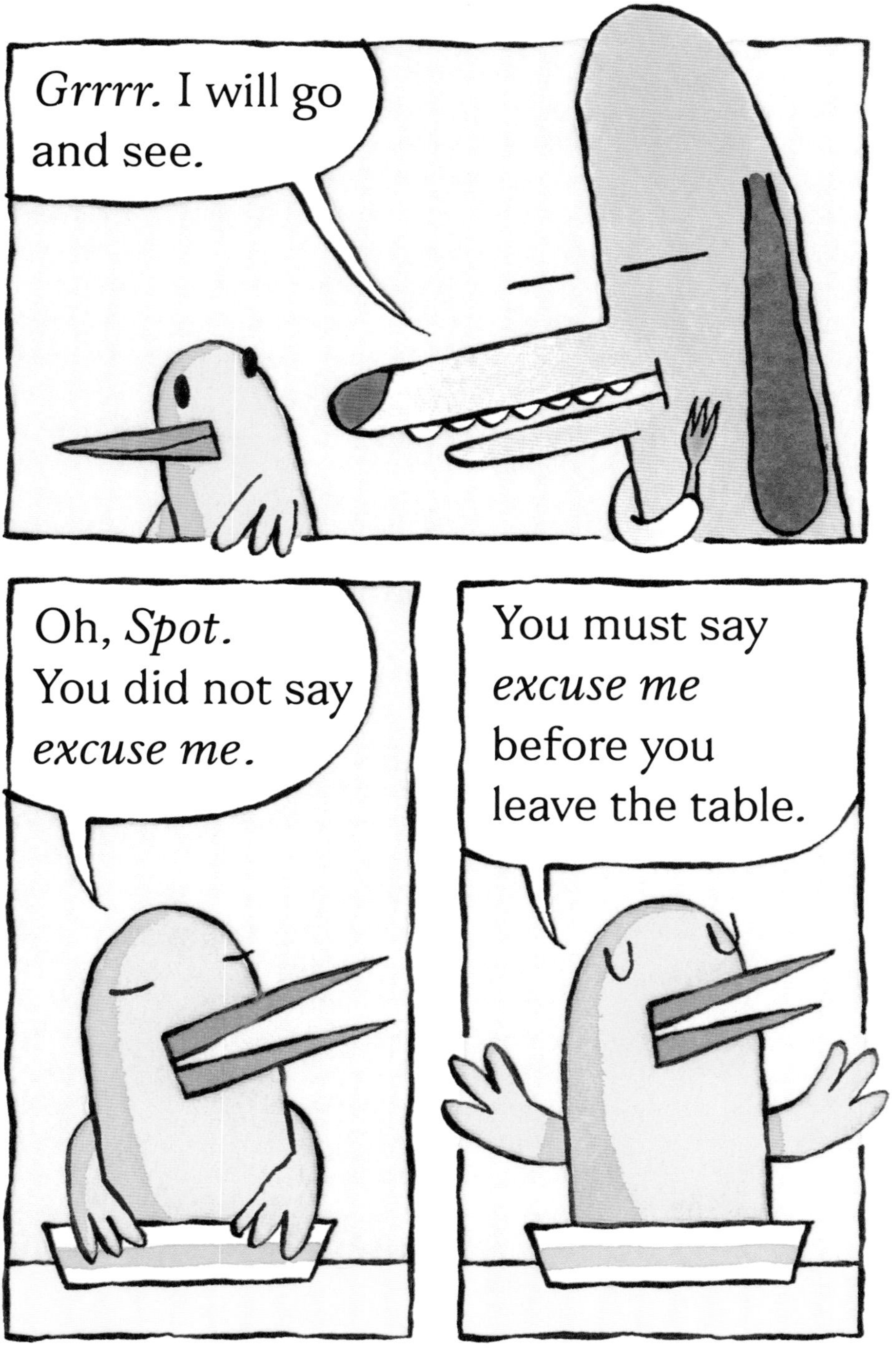
Grrrr. I will go and see.
Oh, *Spot.* You did not say *excuse me.*
You must say *excuse me* before you leave the table.

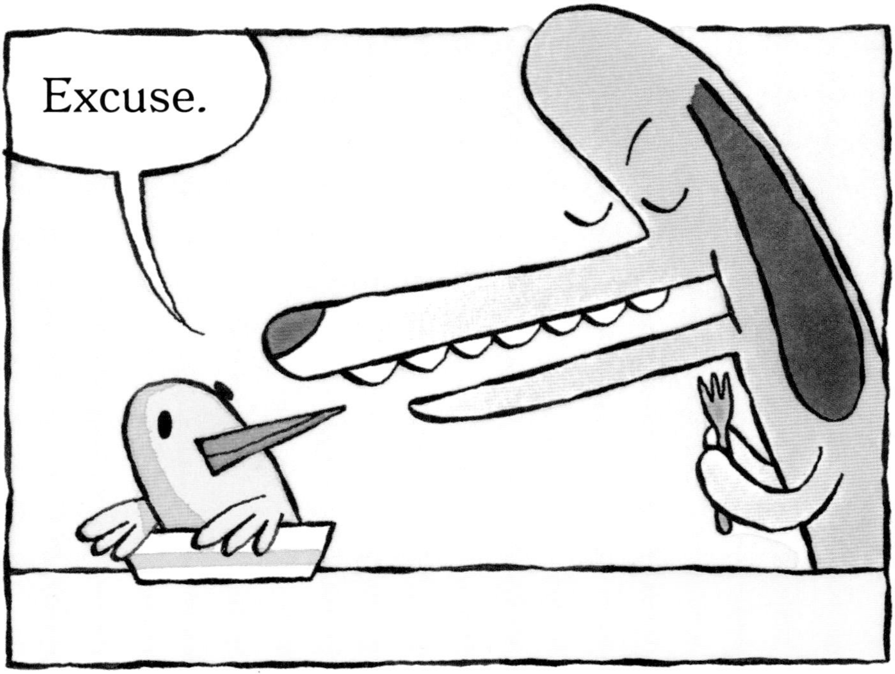
Excuse.

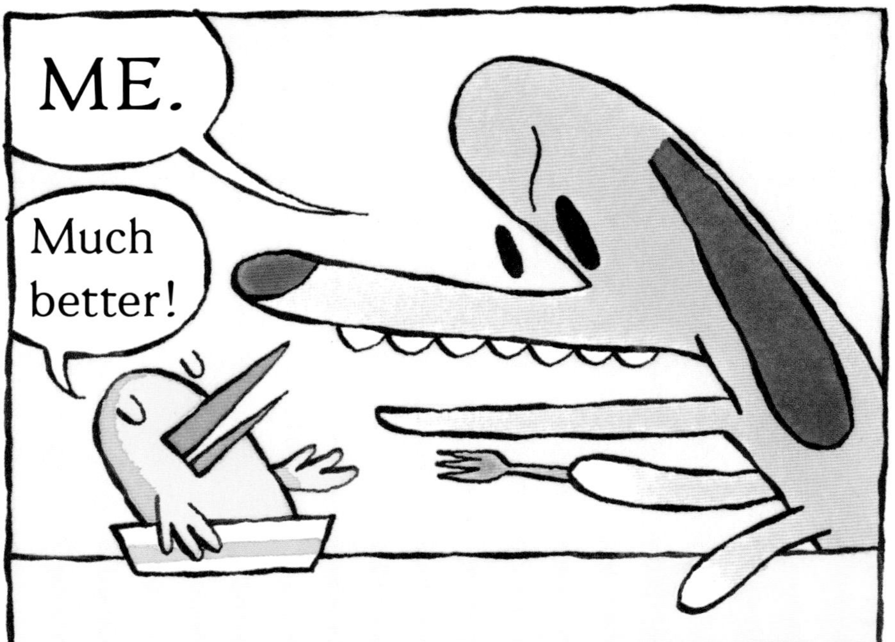
ME.
Much better!

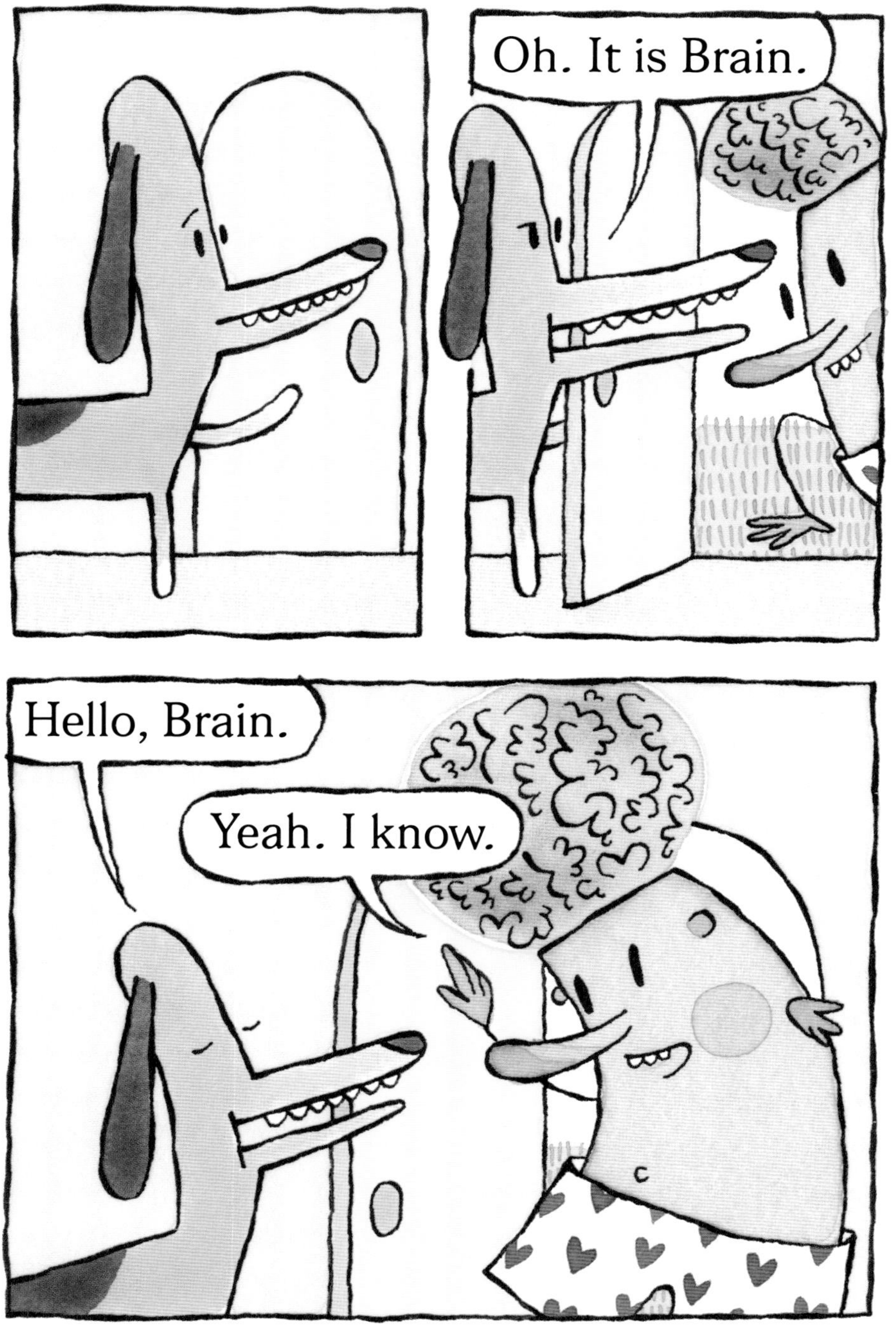

Oh. It is Brain.
Hello, Brain.
Yeah. I know.

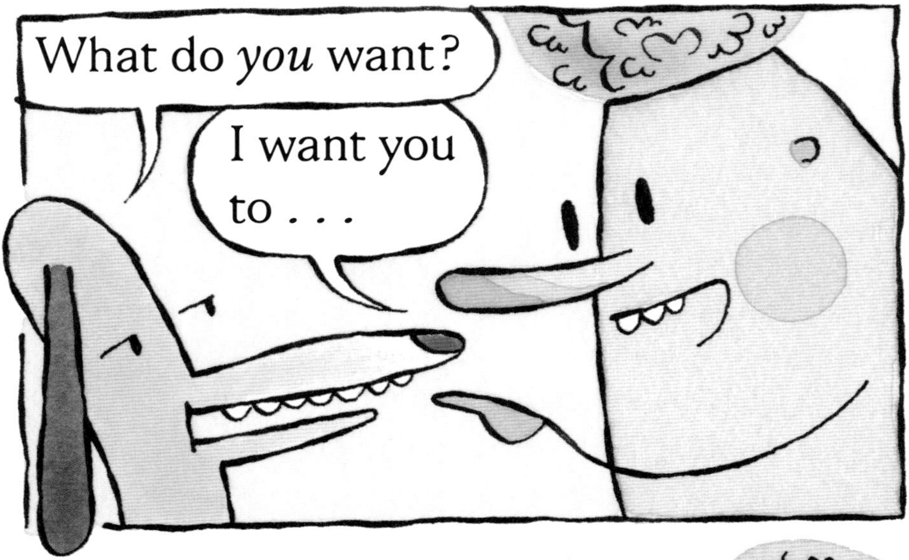
What do *you* want?
I want you to . . .

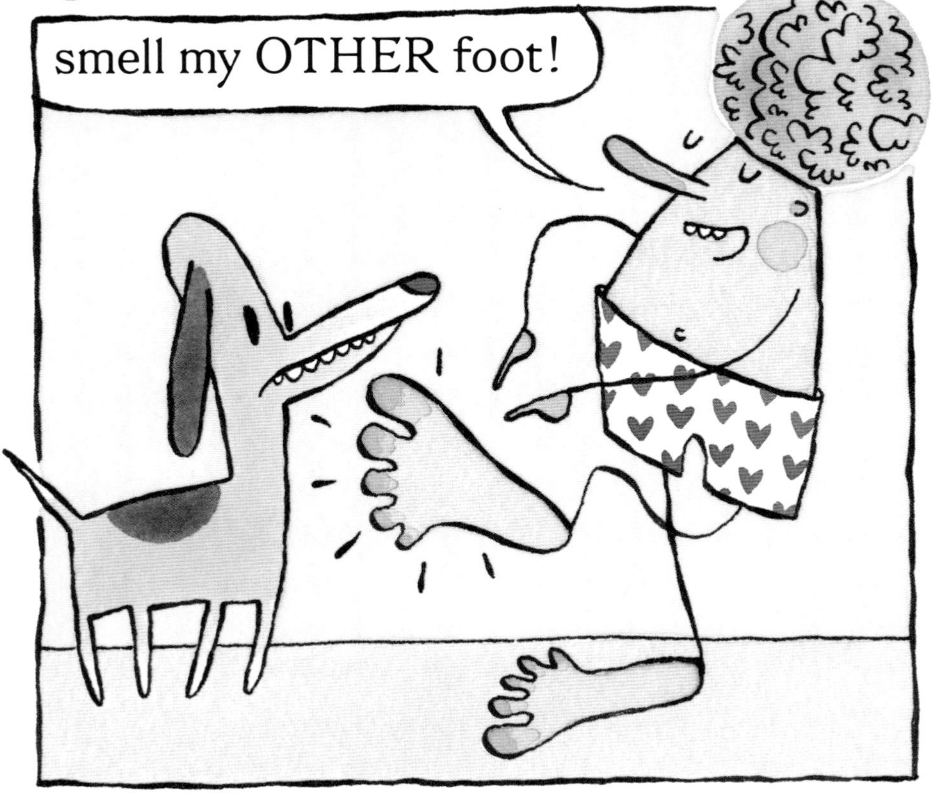
smell my OTHER foot!

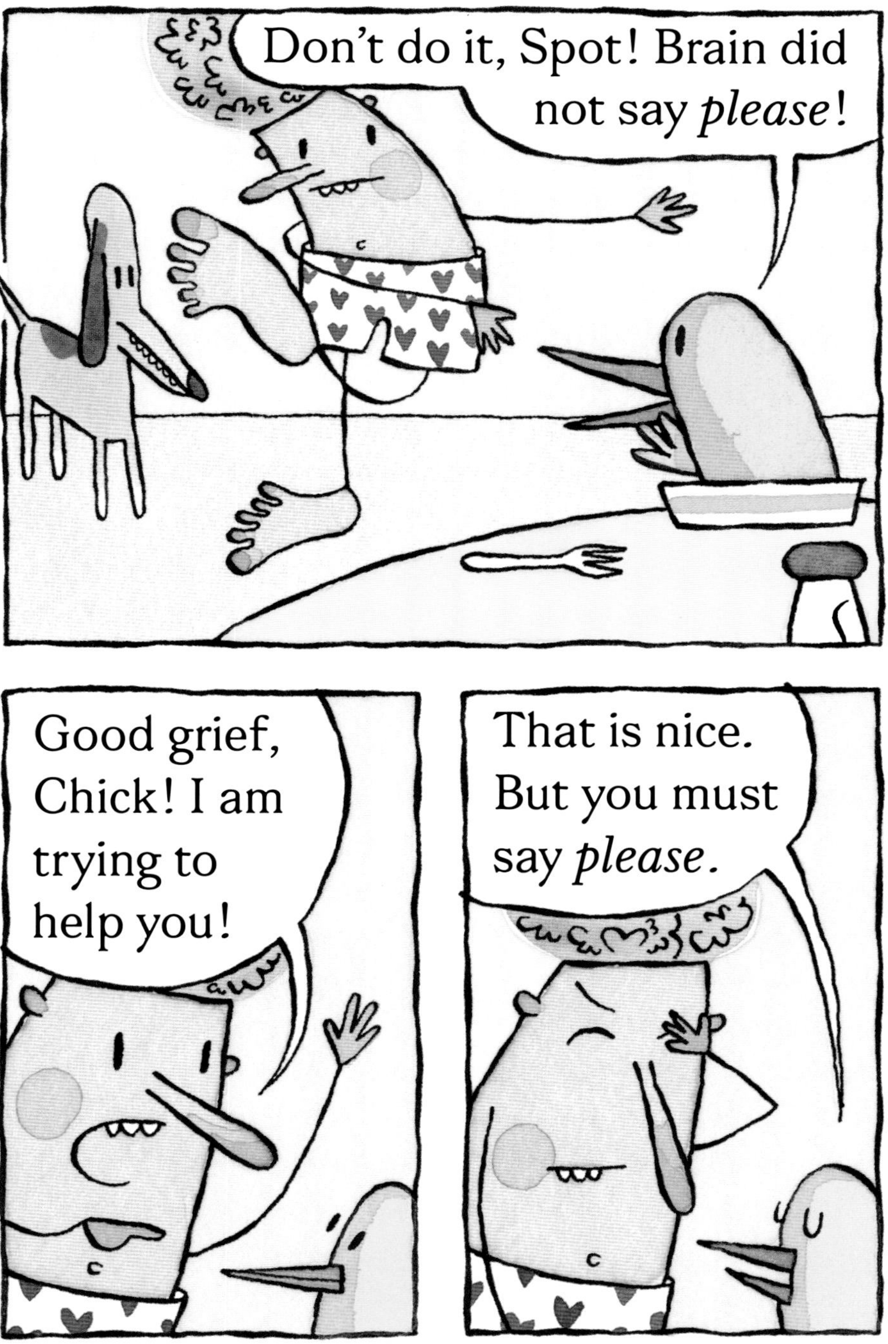
Don't do it, Spot! Brain did not say *please*!
Good grief, Chick! I am trying to help you!
That is nice. But you must say *please*.

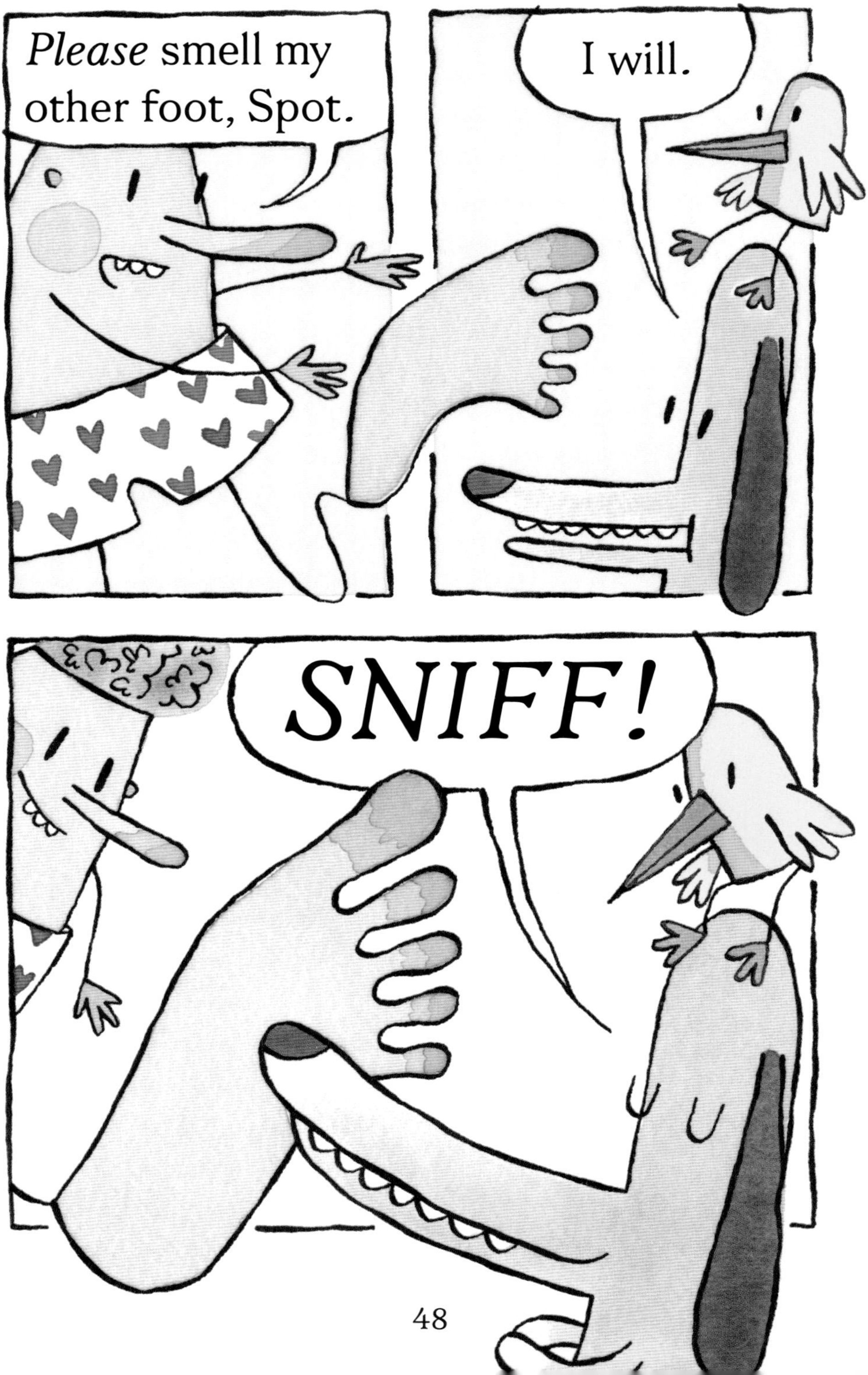
Please smell my other foot, Spot.
I will.
SNIFF!

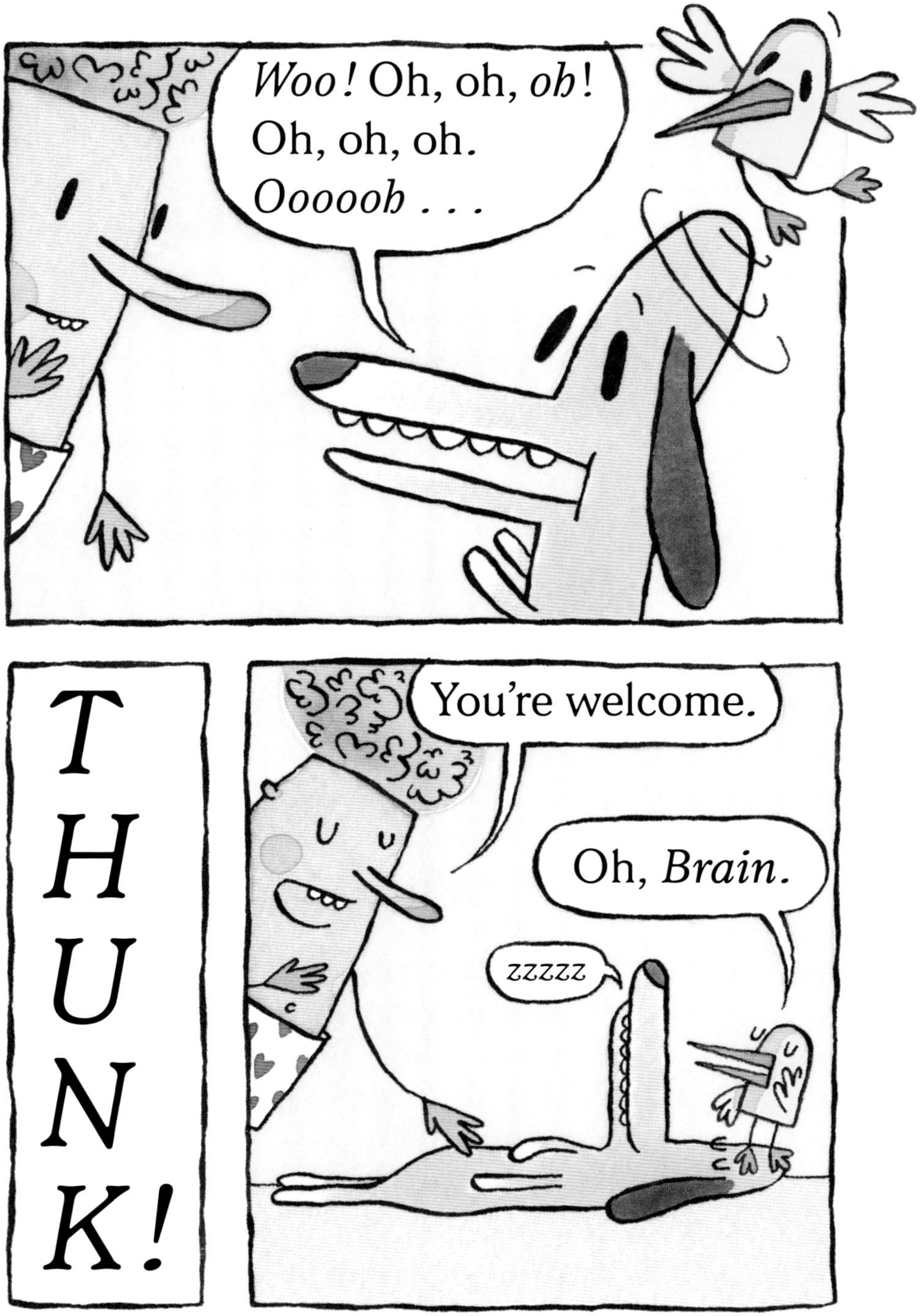
Woo! Oh, oh, *oh*! Oh, oh, oh. *Oooooh . . .*
THUNK!
You're welcome.
Oh, *Brain*.
zzzzz

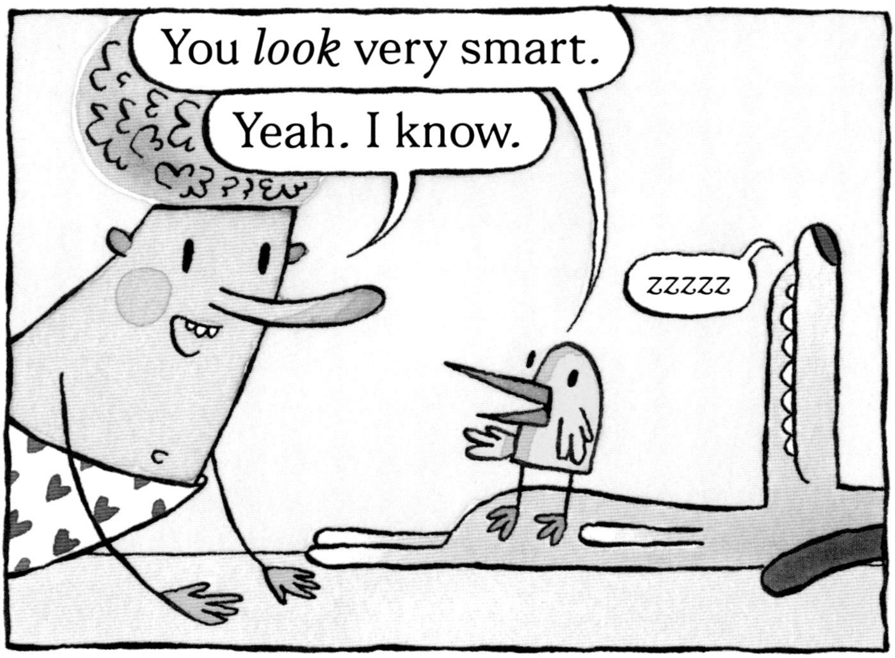
You *look* very smart.
Yeah. I know.
ZZZZZ

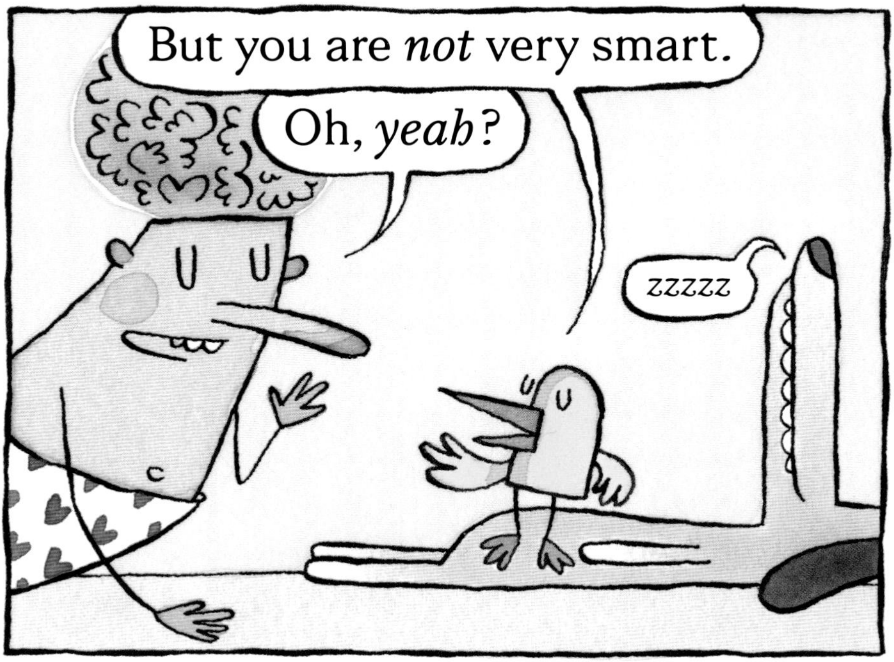
But you are *not* very smart.
Oh, *yeah*?
ZZZZZ

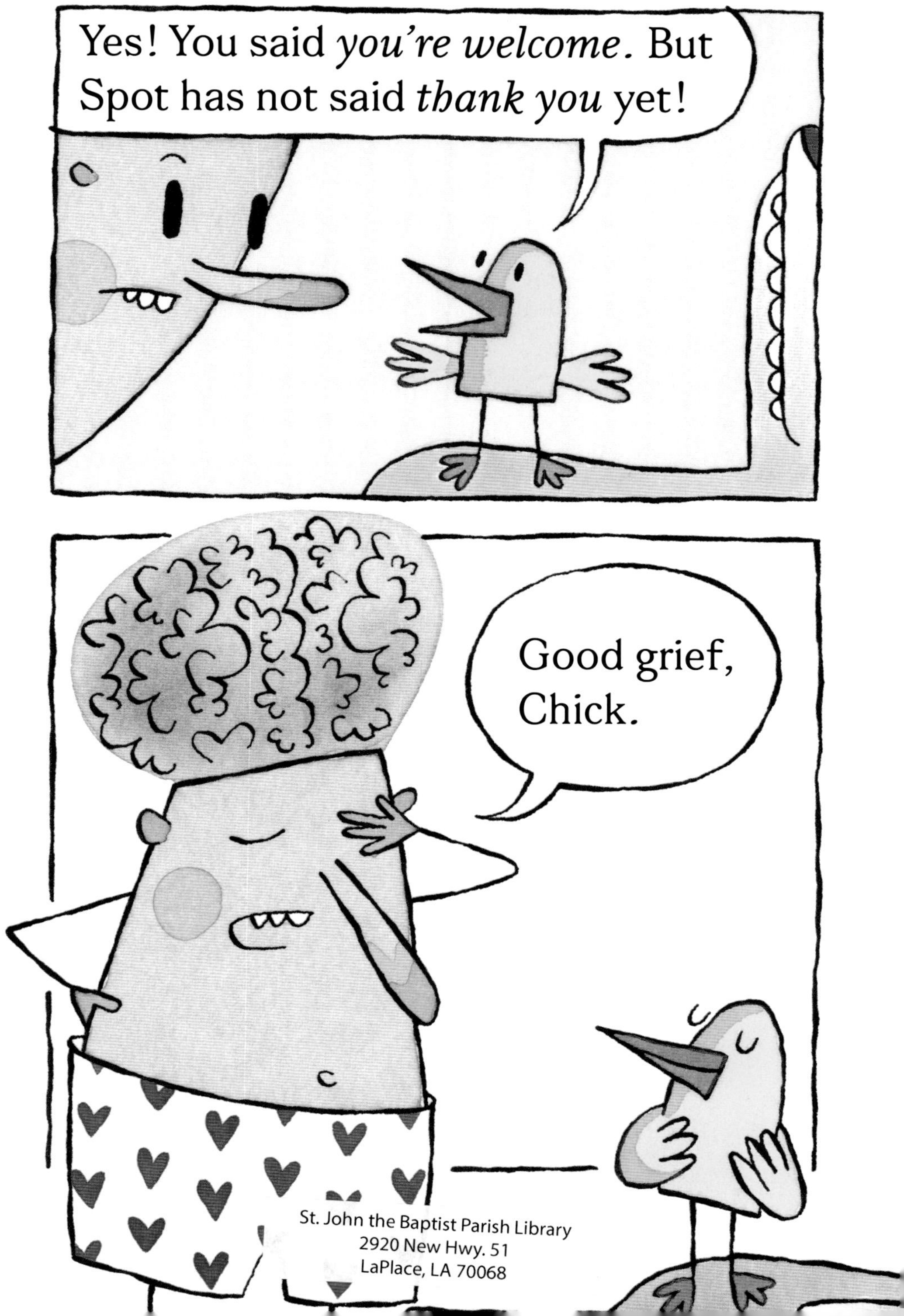
Yes! You said *you're welcome.* But Spot has not said *thank you* yet!
Good grief, Chick.

Chapter 4

Other Foot

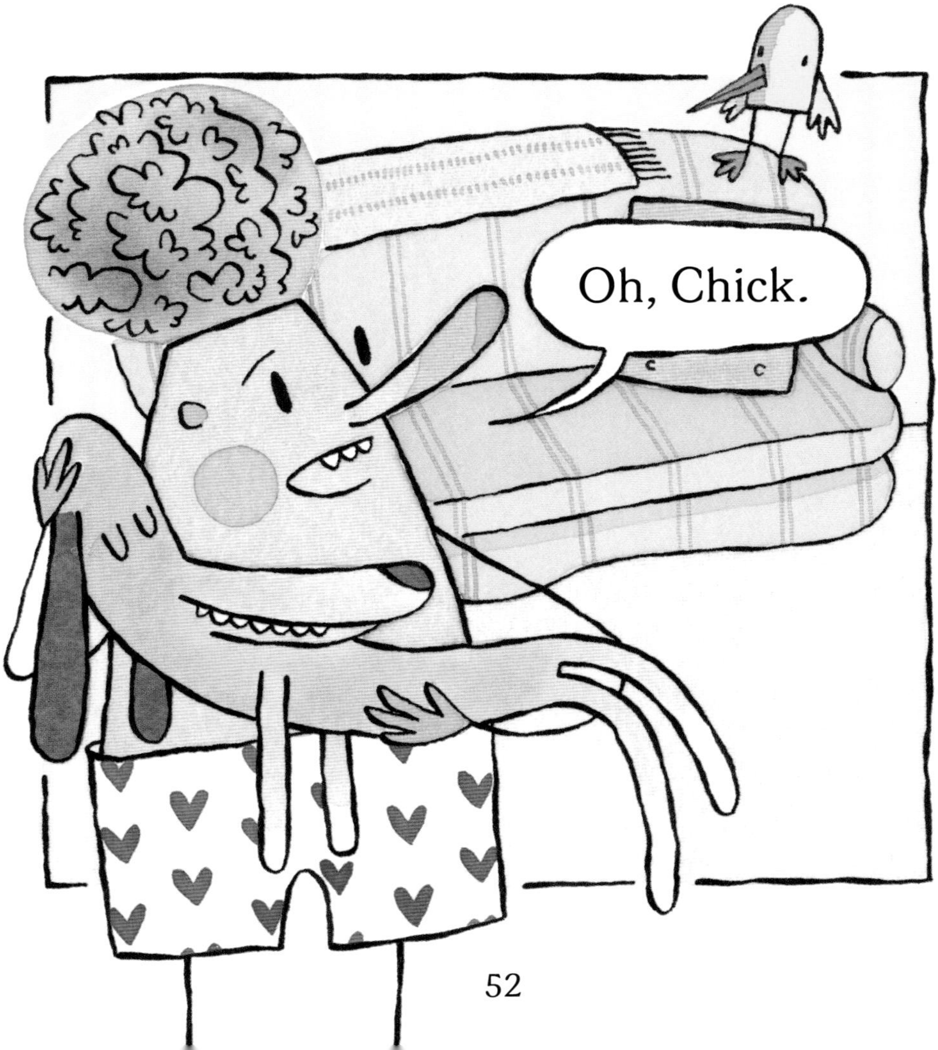
Oh, Chick.

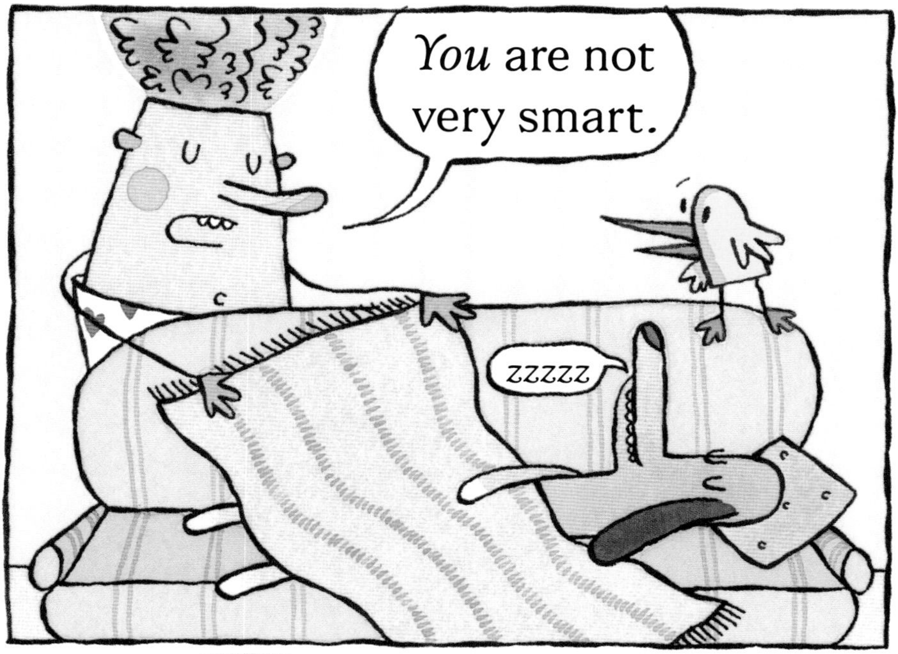
You are not very smart.
zzzzz

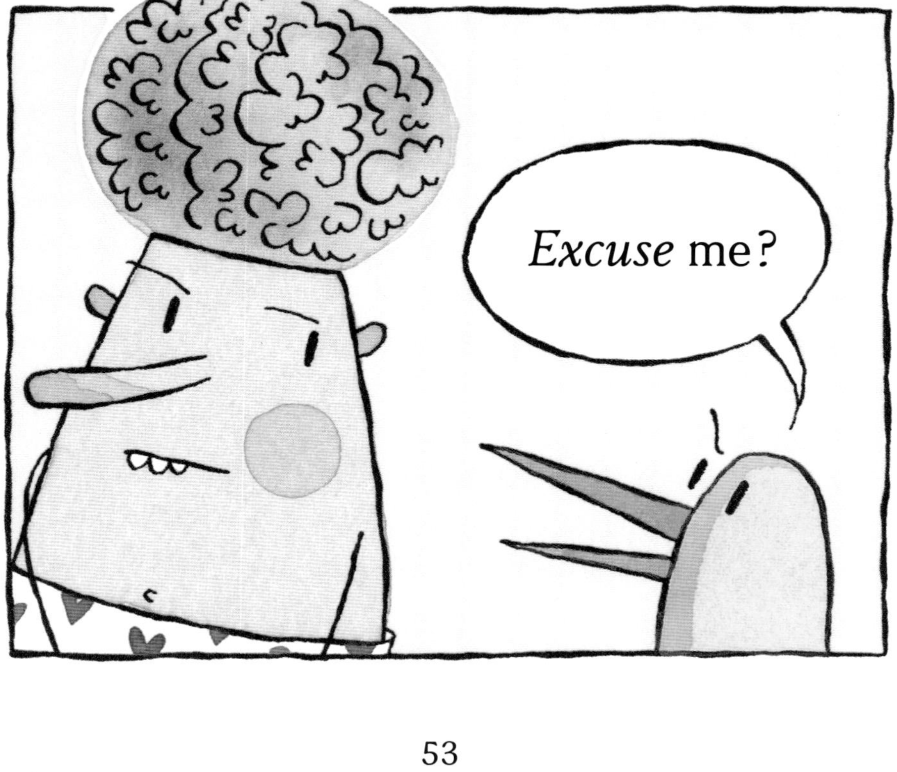
Excuse me?

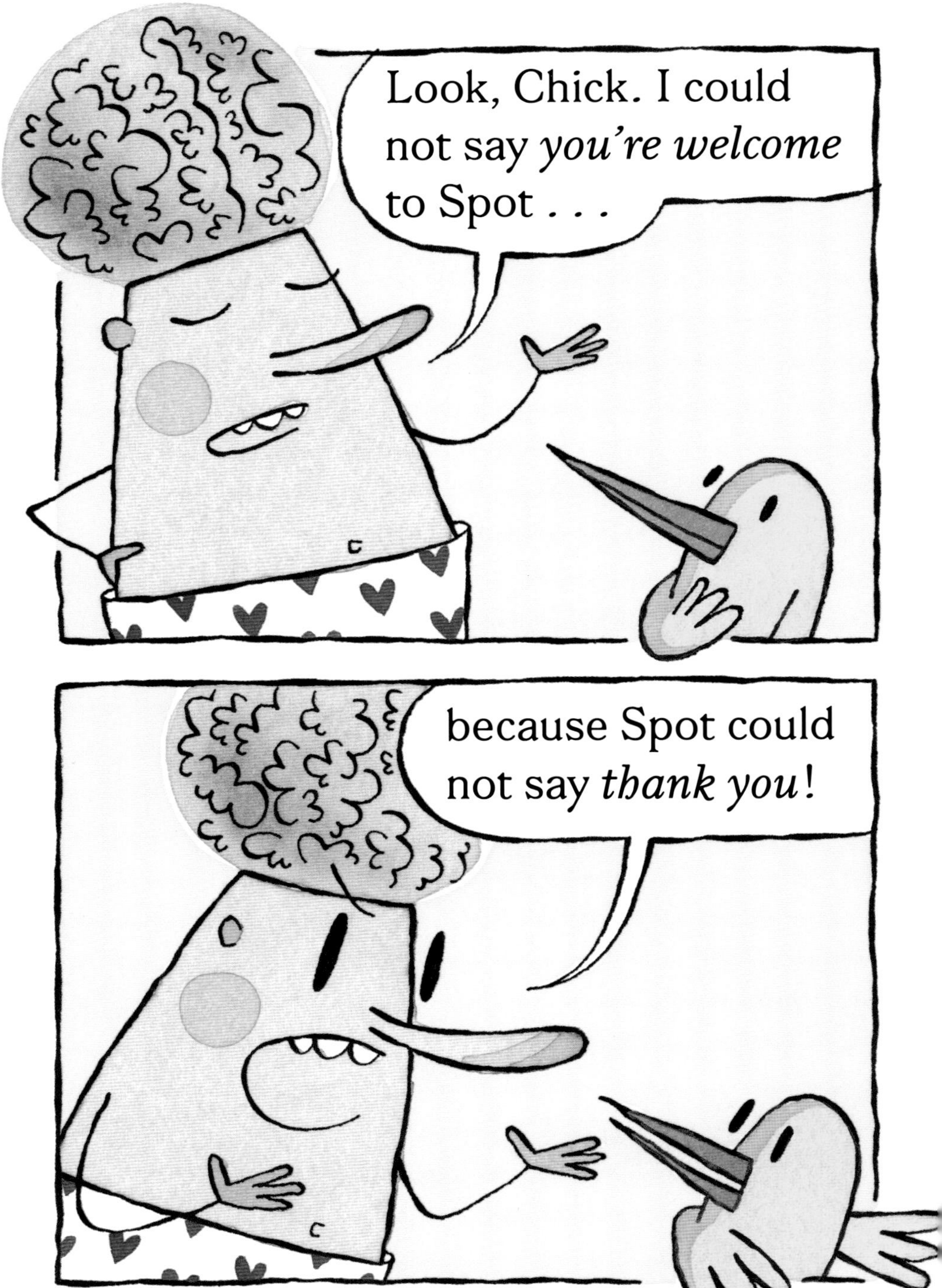
Look, Chick. I could not say *you're welcome* to Spot . . .
because Spot could not say *thank you*!

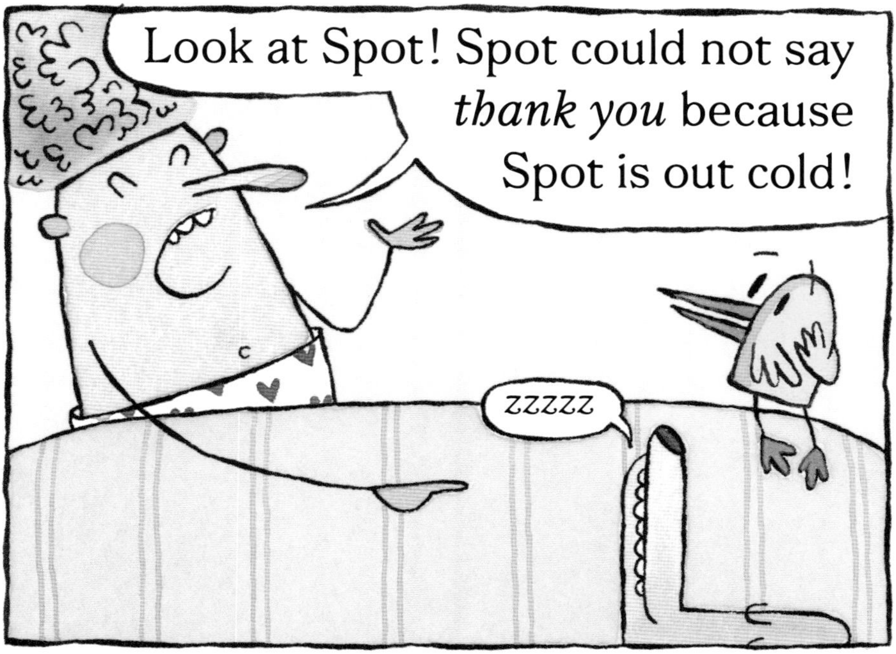
Look at Spot! Spot could not say *thank you* because Spot is out cold!
ZZZZZ

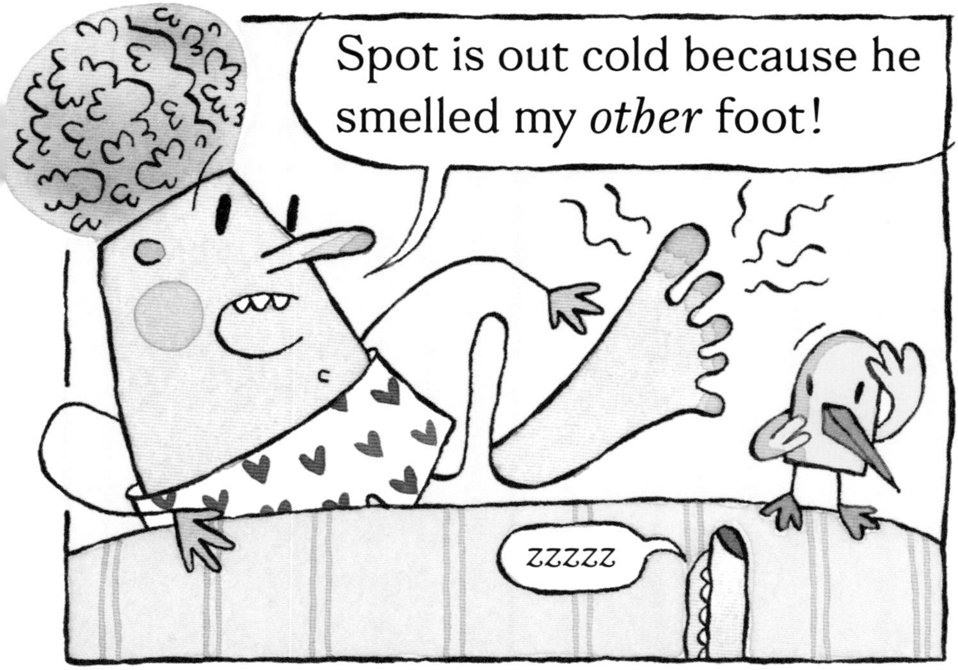
Spot is out cold because he smelled my *other* foot!
ZZZZZ

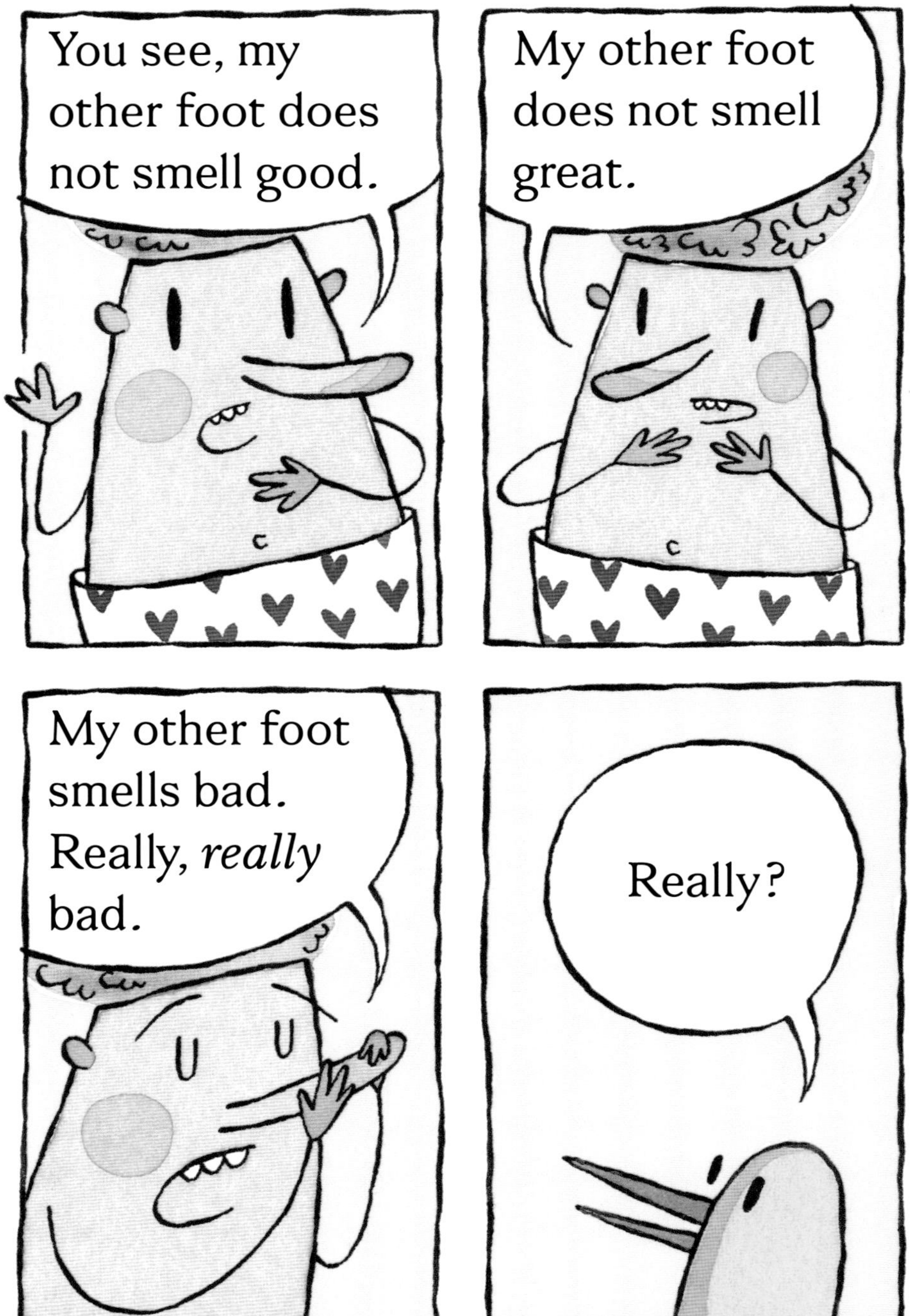
You see, my other foot does not smell good.
My other foot does not smell great.
My other foot smells bad. Really, *really* bad.
Really?

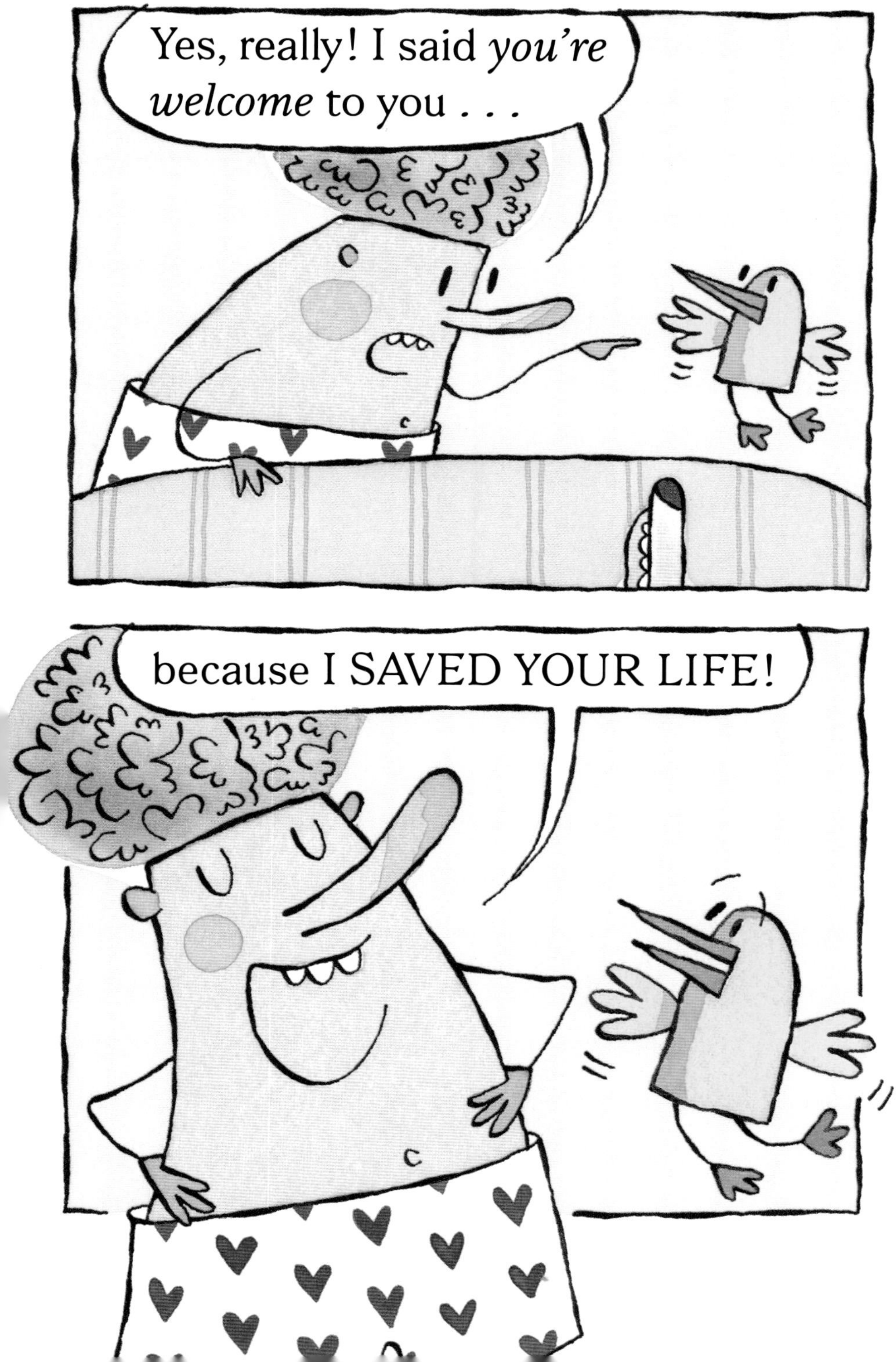
Yes, really! I said *you're welcome* to you . . .
because I SAVED YOUR LIFE!

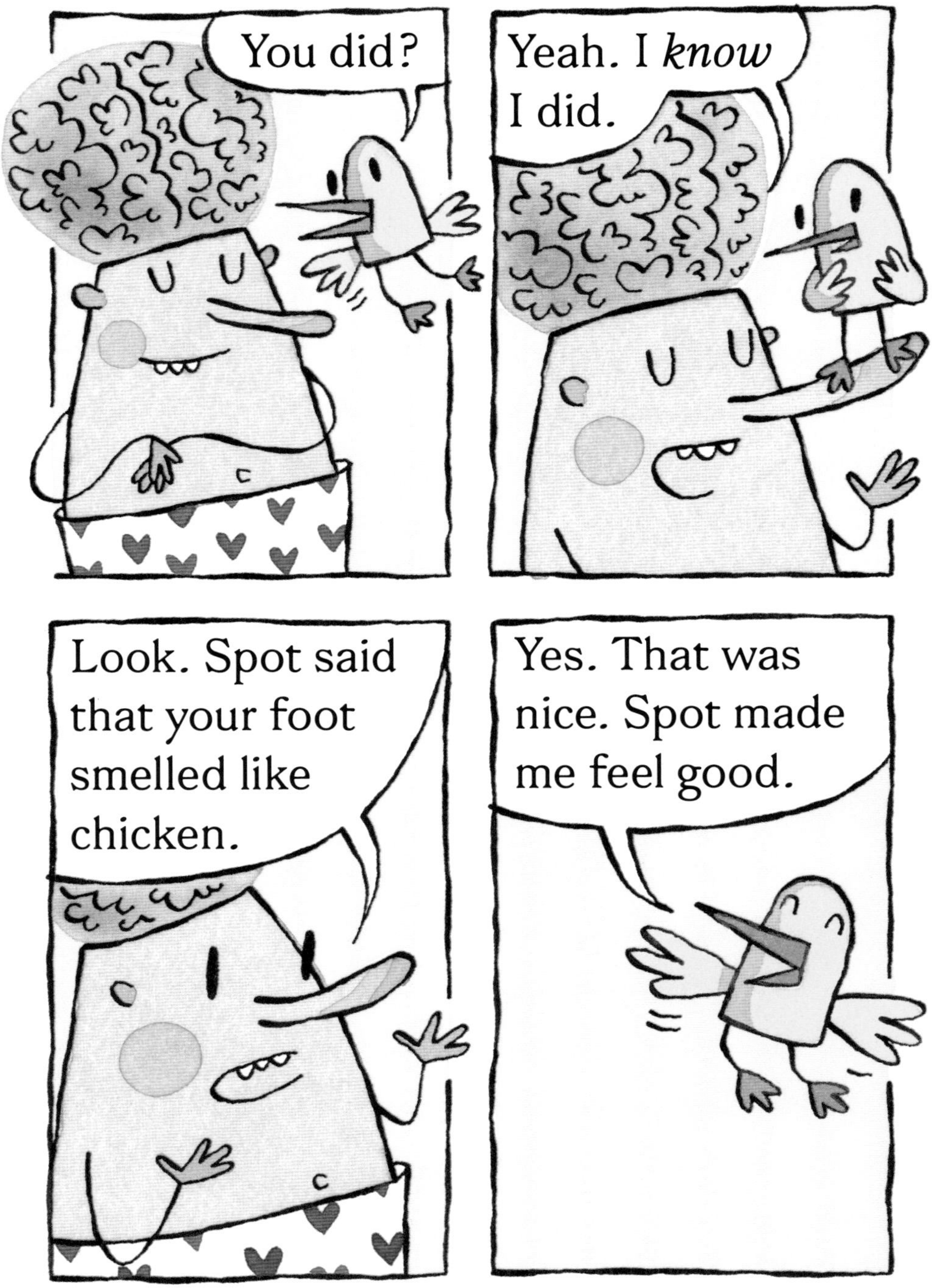
You did?
Yeah. I *know* I did.
Look. Spot said that your foot smelled like chicken.
Yes. That was nice. Spot made me feel good.

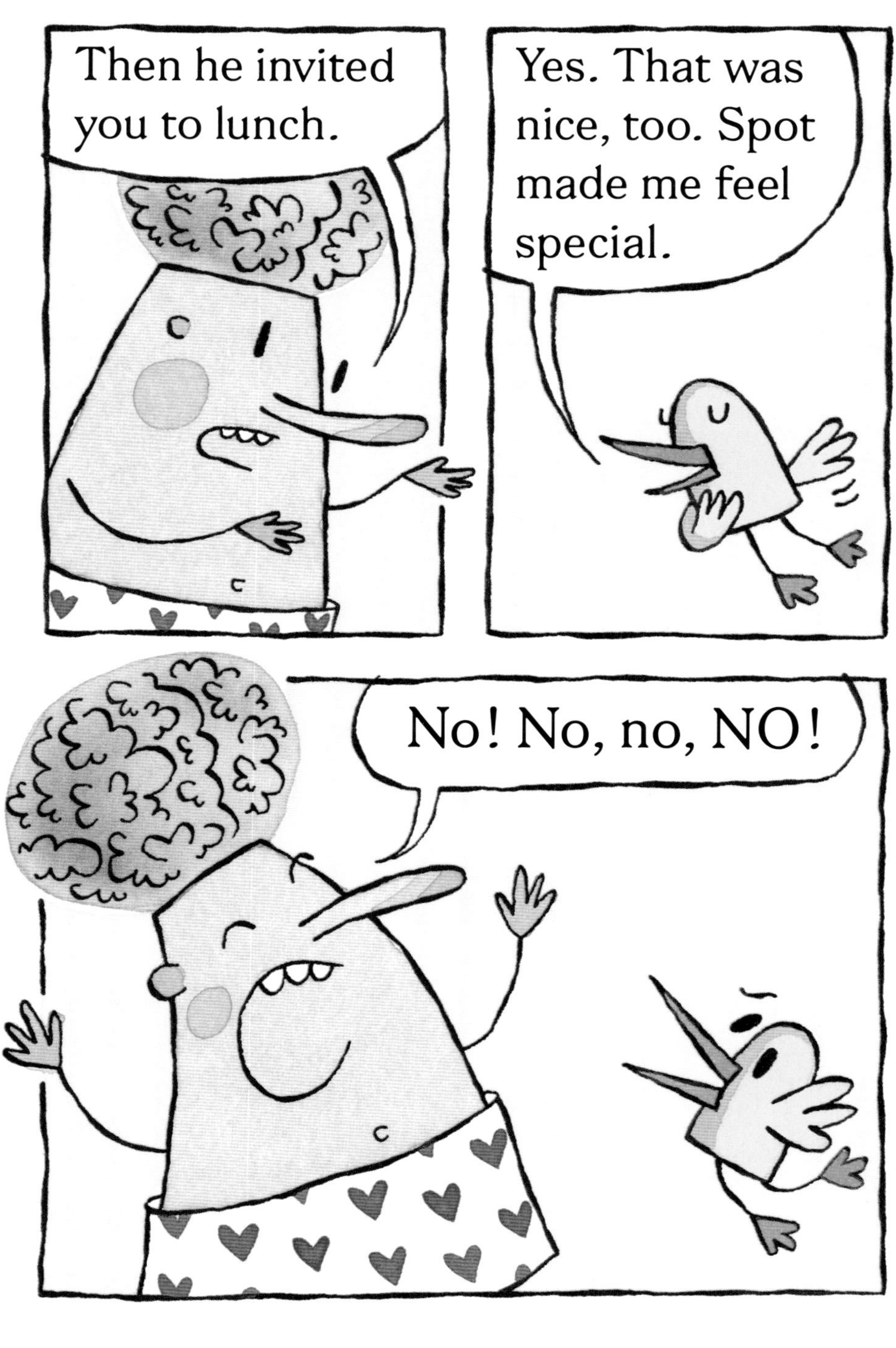
Then he invited you to lunch.
Yes. That was nice, too. Spot made me feel special.
No! No, no, NO!

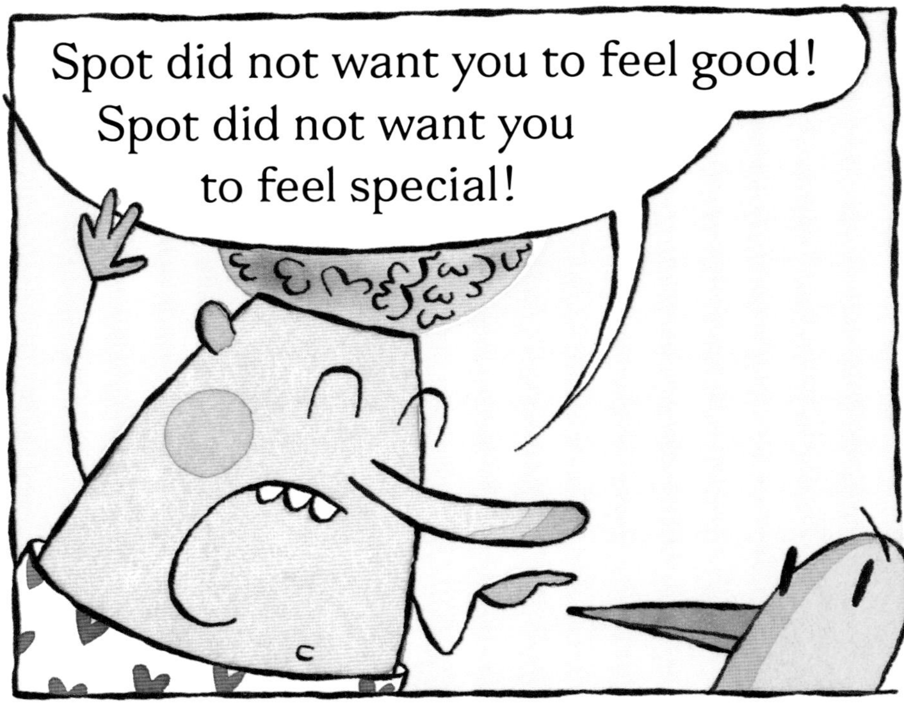
Spot did not want you to feel good! Spot did not want you to feel special!

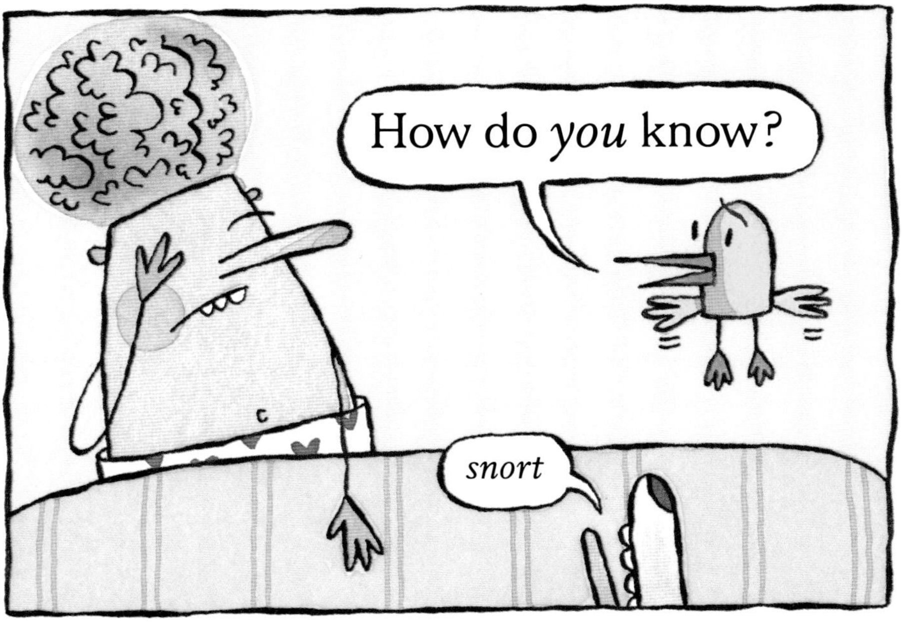
How do *you* know?
snort

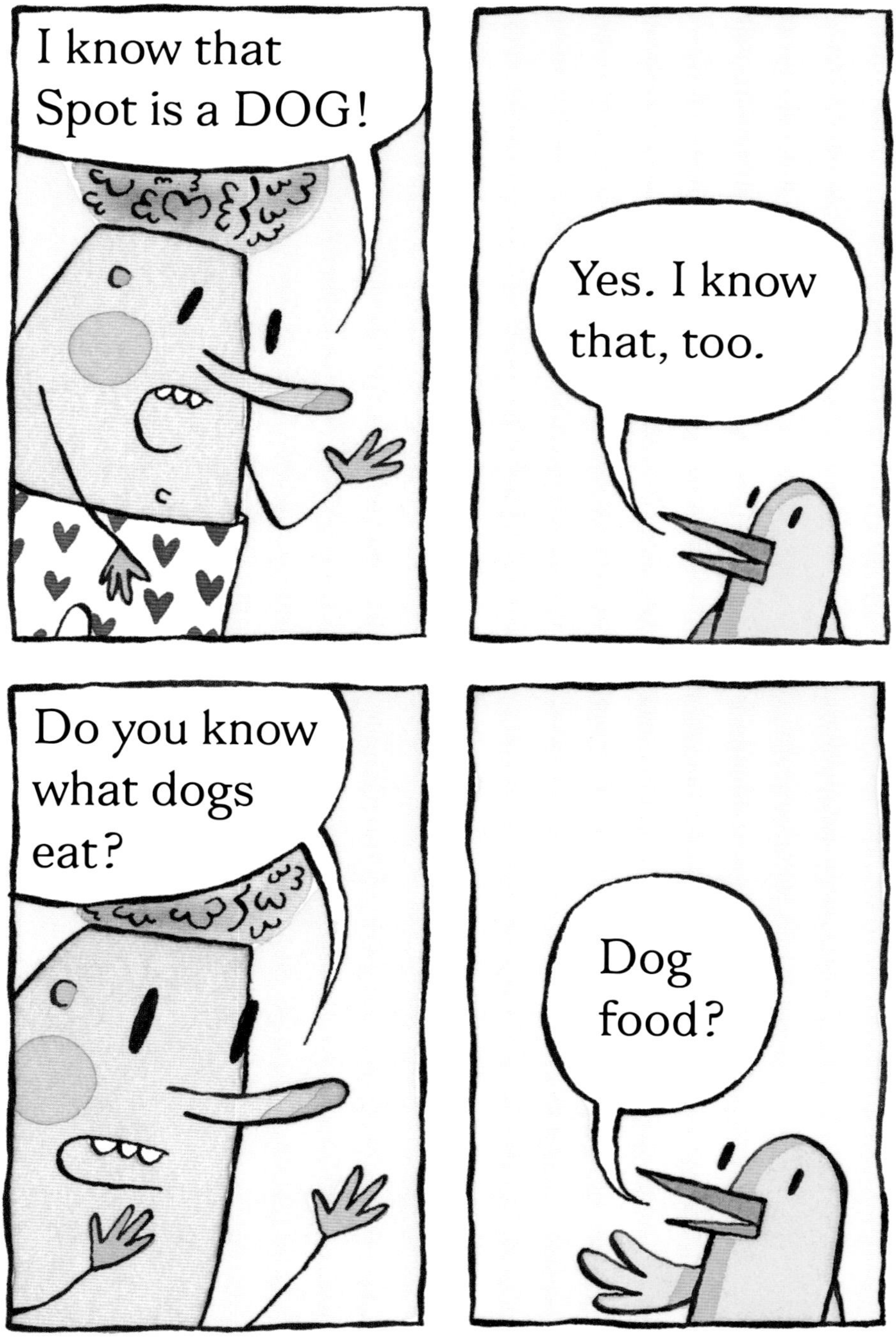
I know that Spot is a DOG!
Yes. I know that, too.
Do you know what dogs eat?
Dog food?

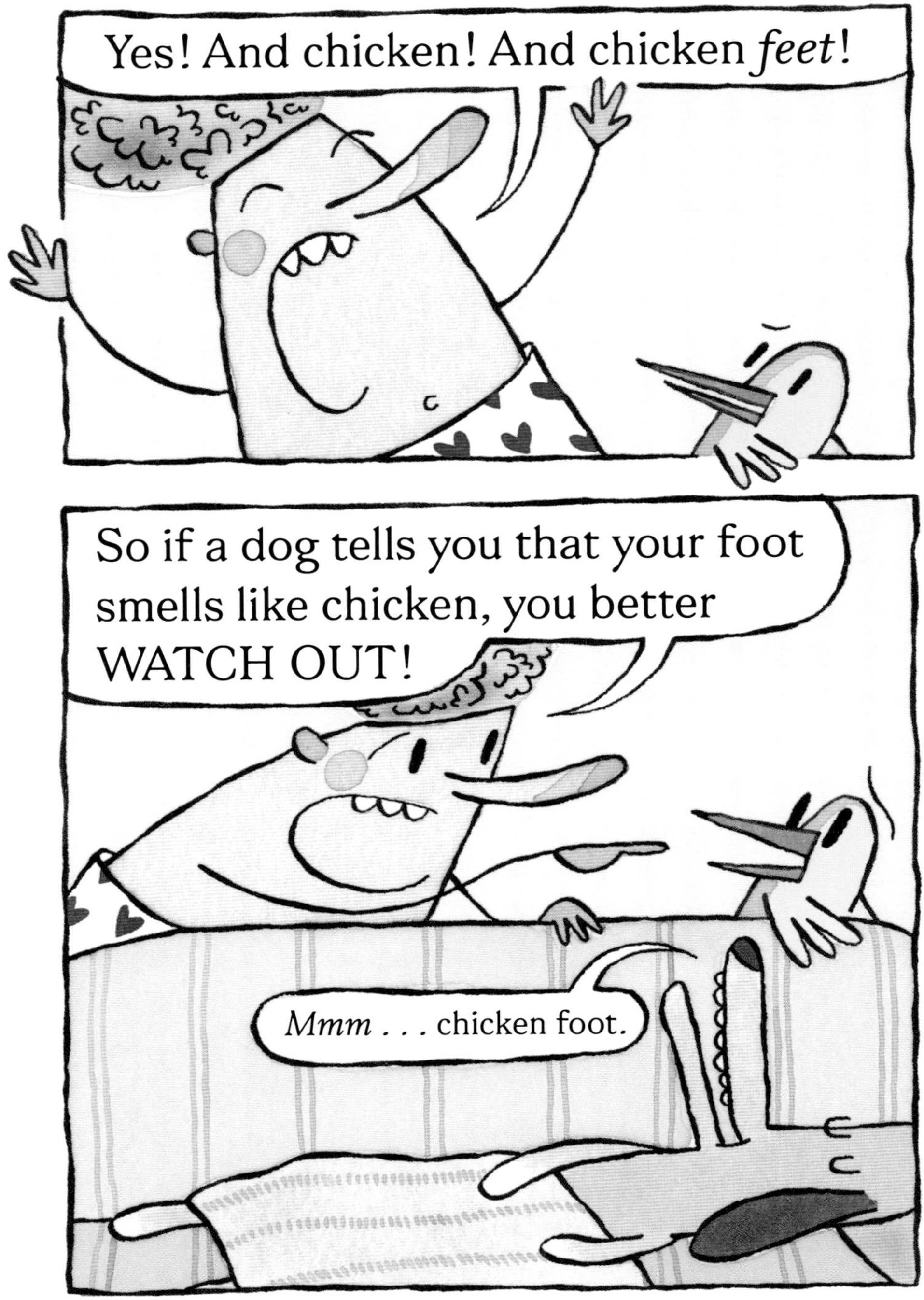
Yes! And chicken! And chicken *feet*!
So if a dog tells you that your foot smells like chicken, you better WATCH OUT!
Mmm . . . chicken foot.

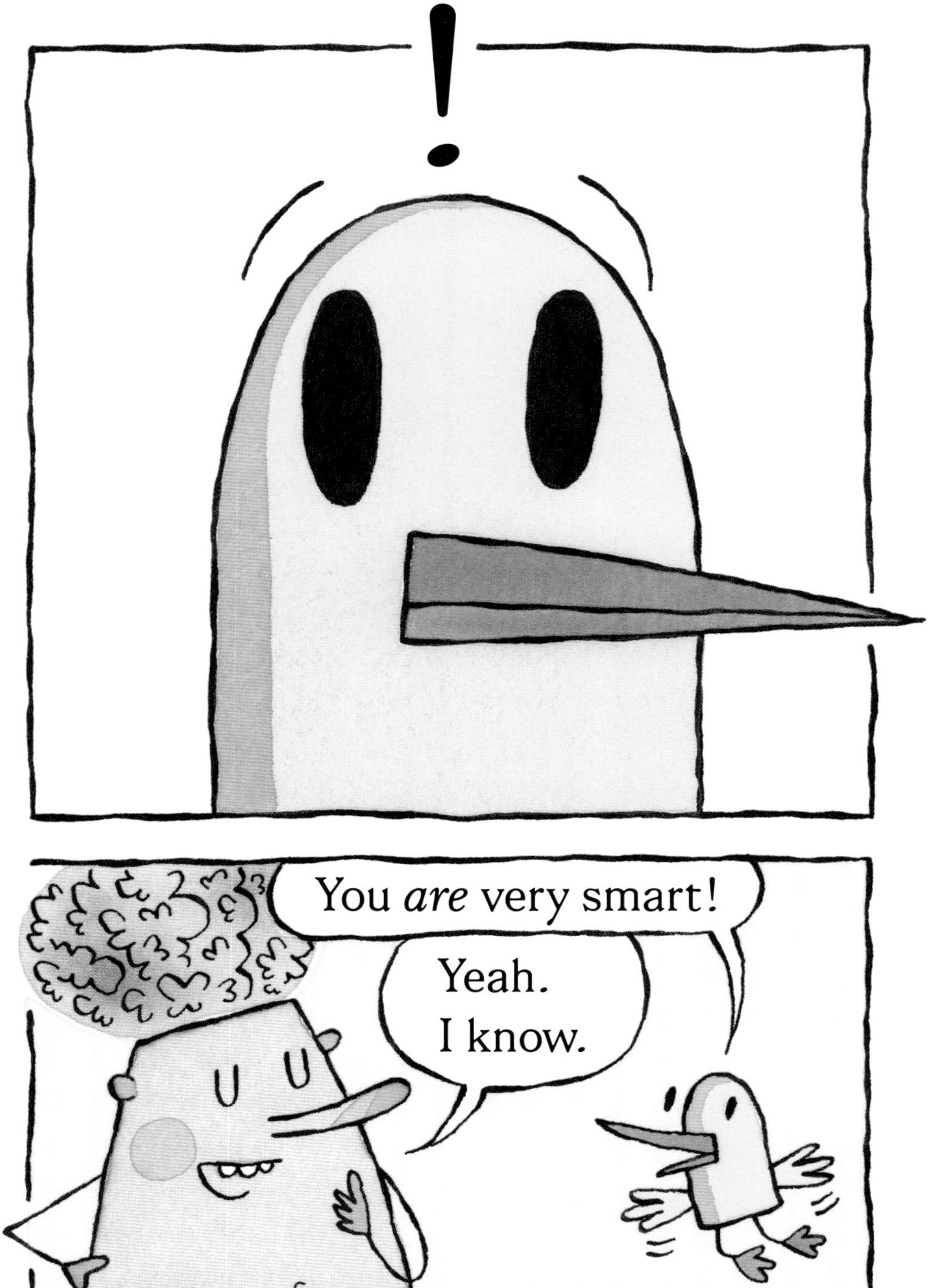
!
You *are* very smart!
Yeah.
I know.

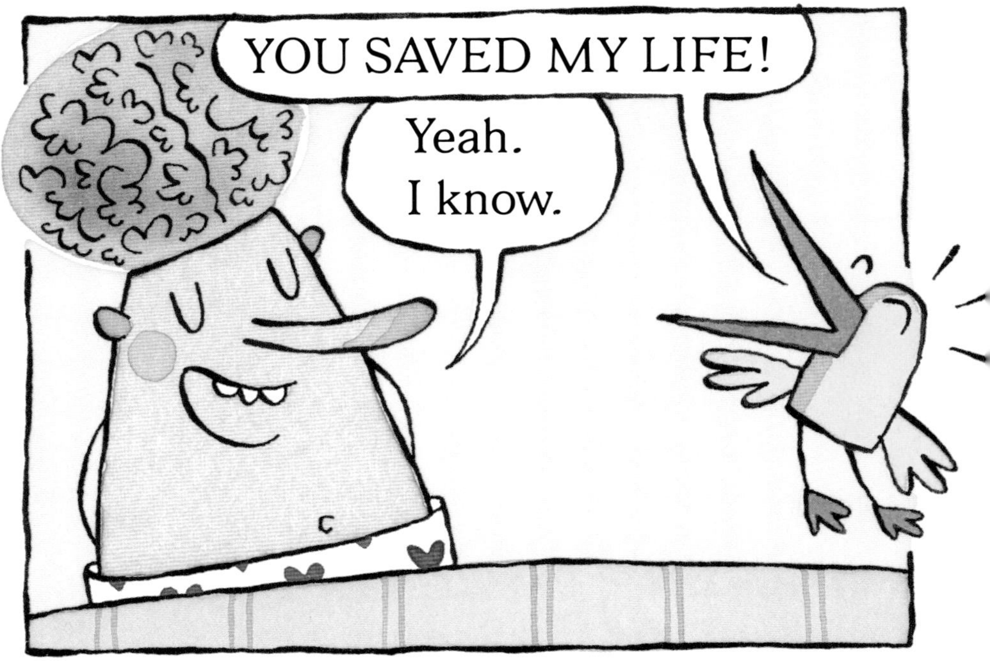
YOU SAVED MY LIFE!
Yeah. I know.

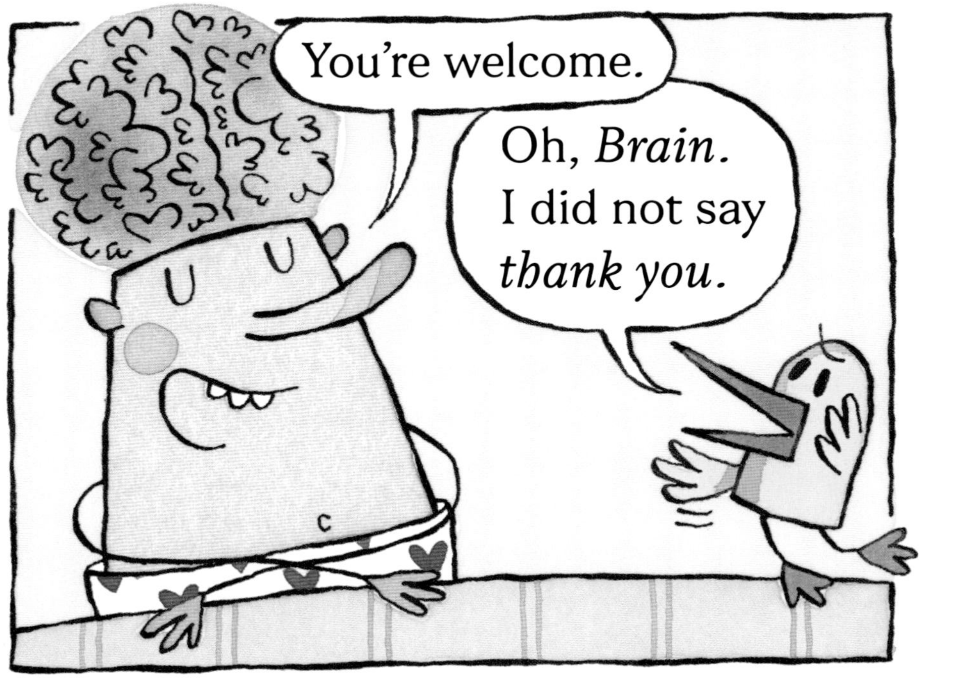
You're welcome.
Oh, *Brain*. I did not say *thank you*.

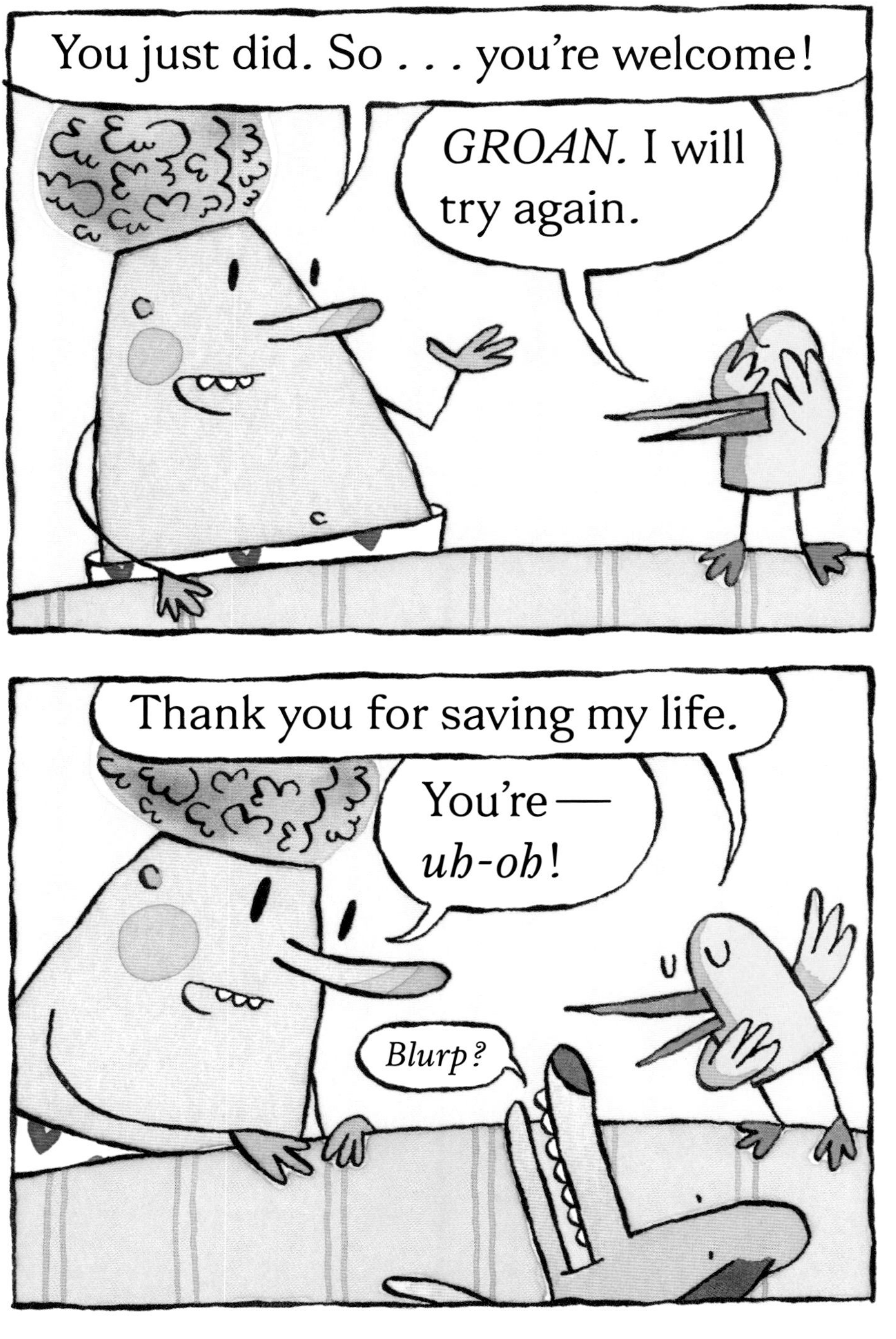
You just did. So . . . you're welcome!
GROAN. I will try again.
Thank you for saving my life.
You're—*uh-oh*!
Blurp?

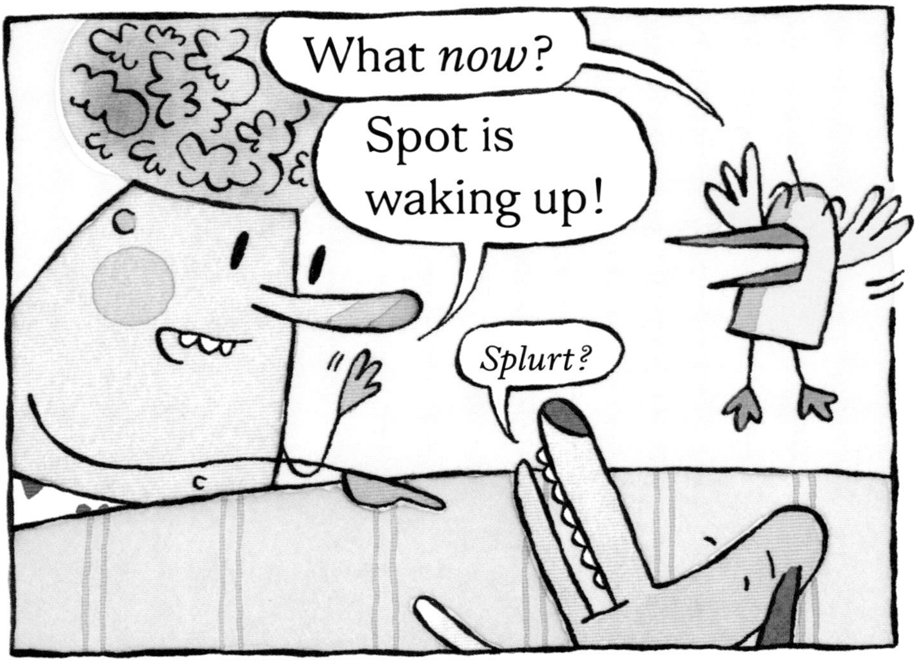
What *now*?
Spot is waking up!
Splurt?

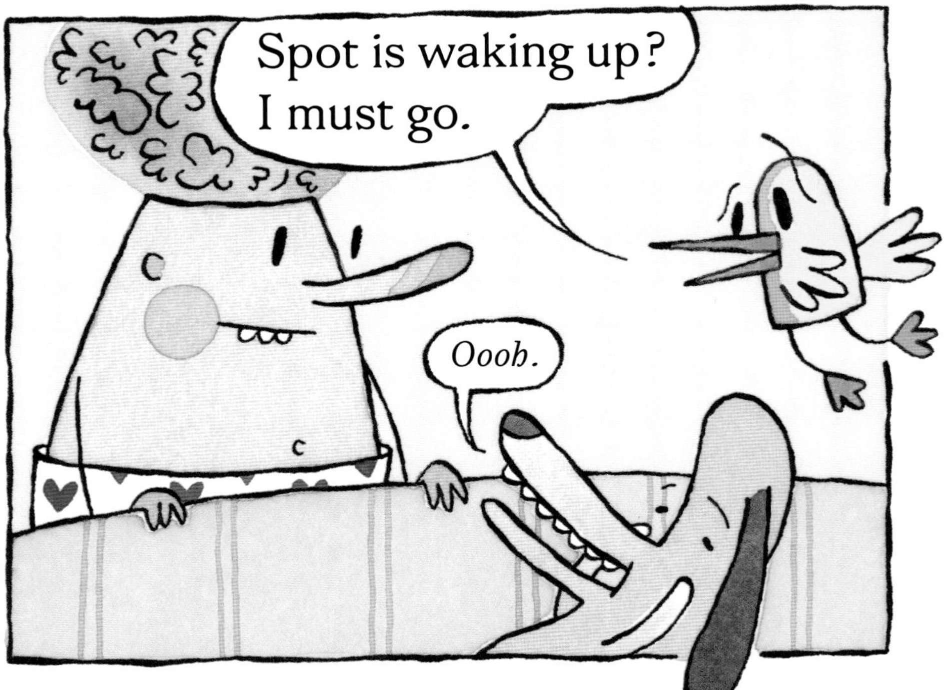
Spot is waking up? I must go.
Oooh.

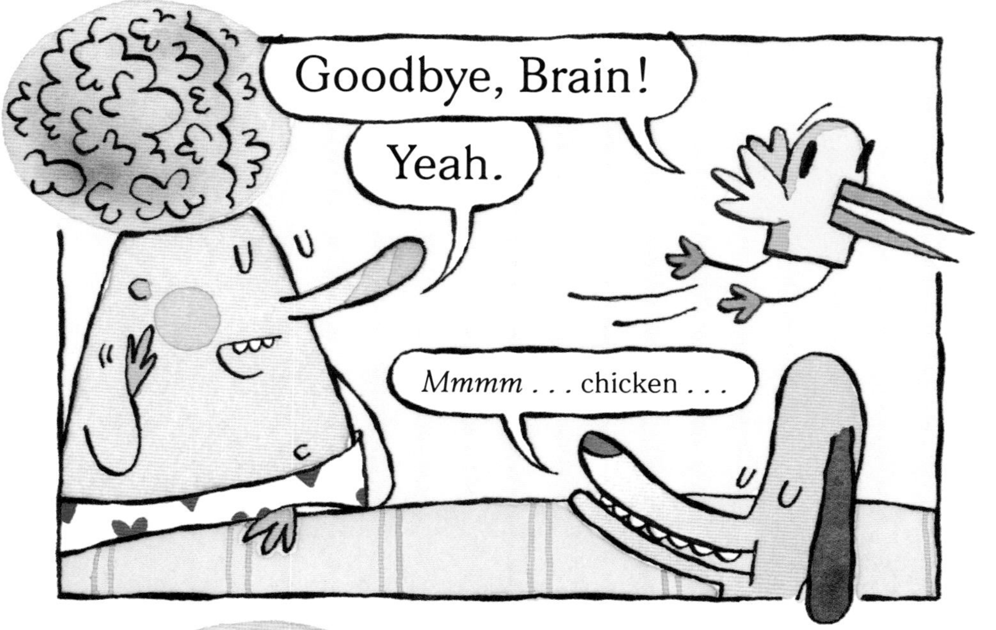
Goodbye, Brain!
Yeah.
Mmmm . . . chicken . . .

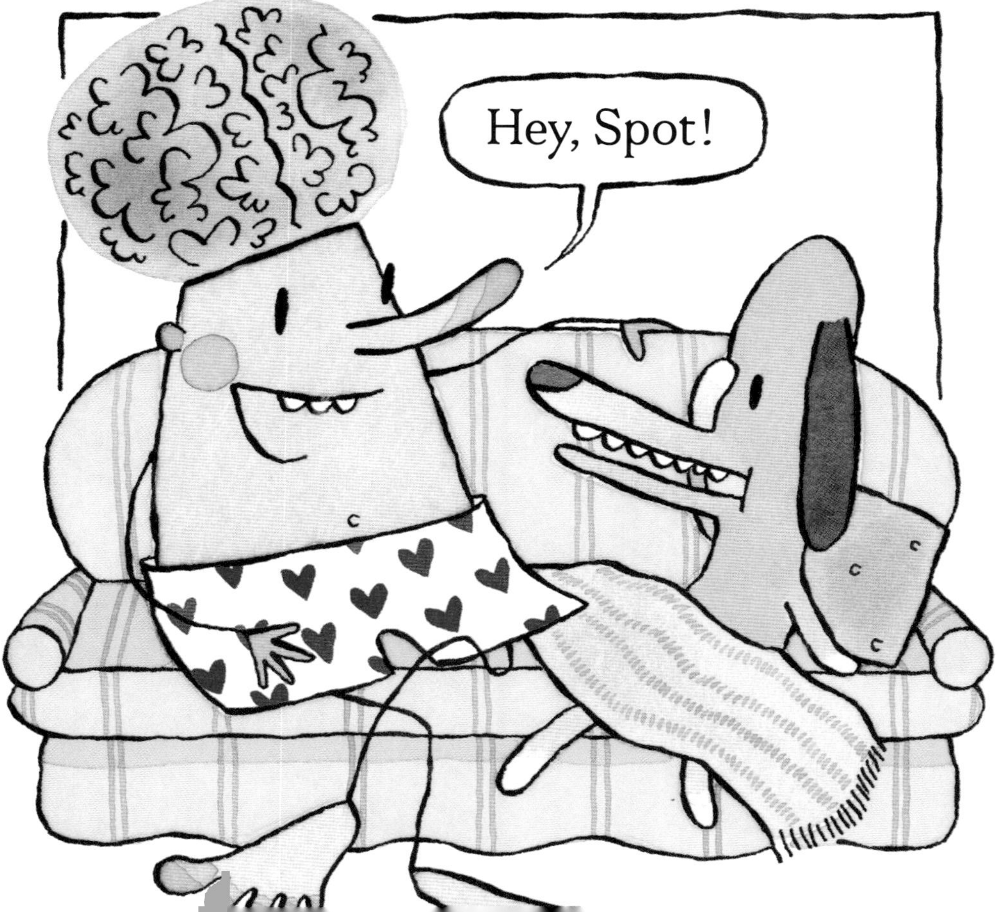
Hey, Spot!

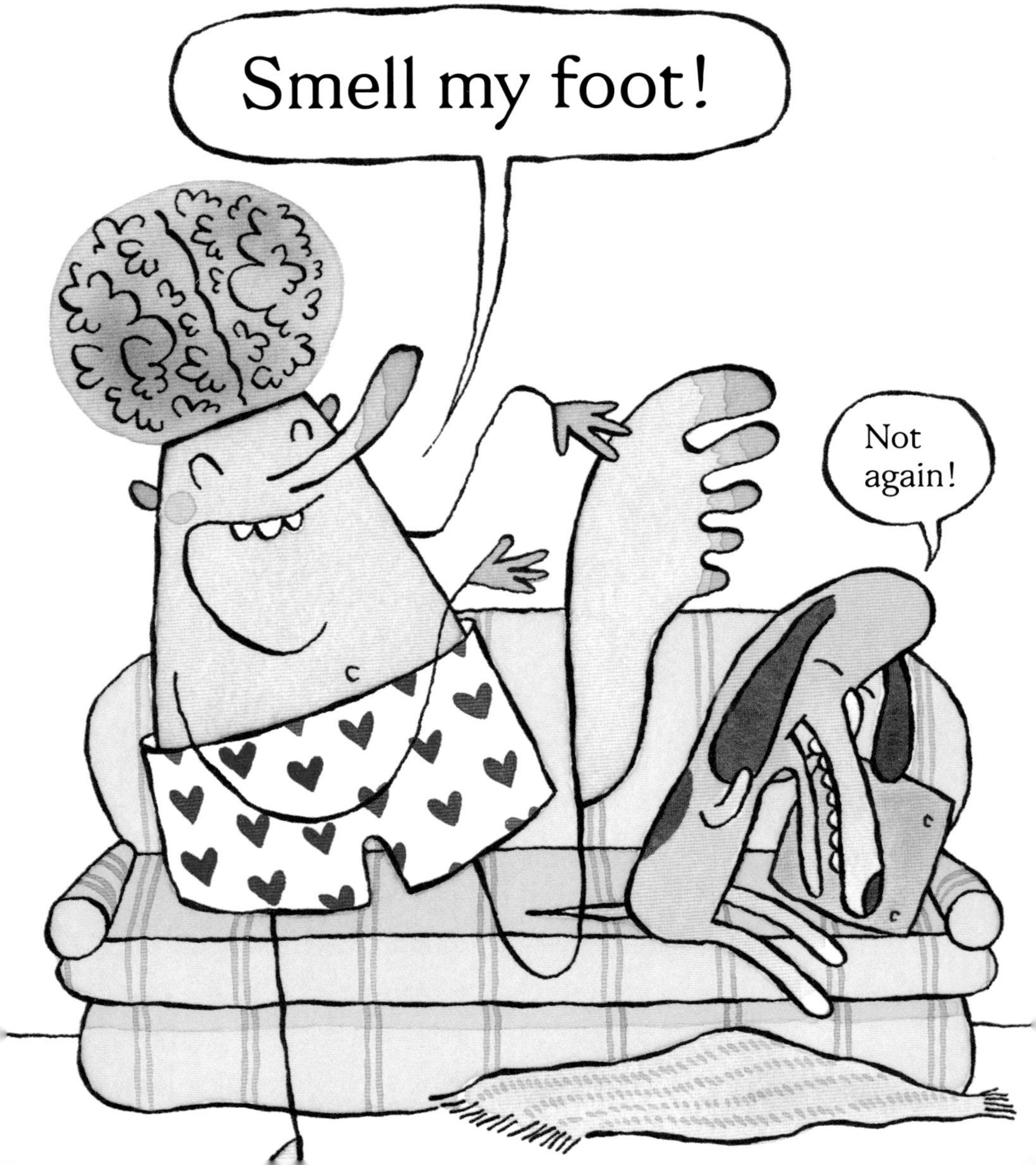
Smell my foot!
Not again!

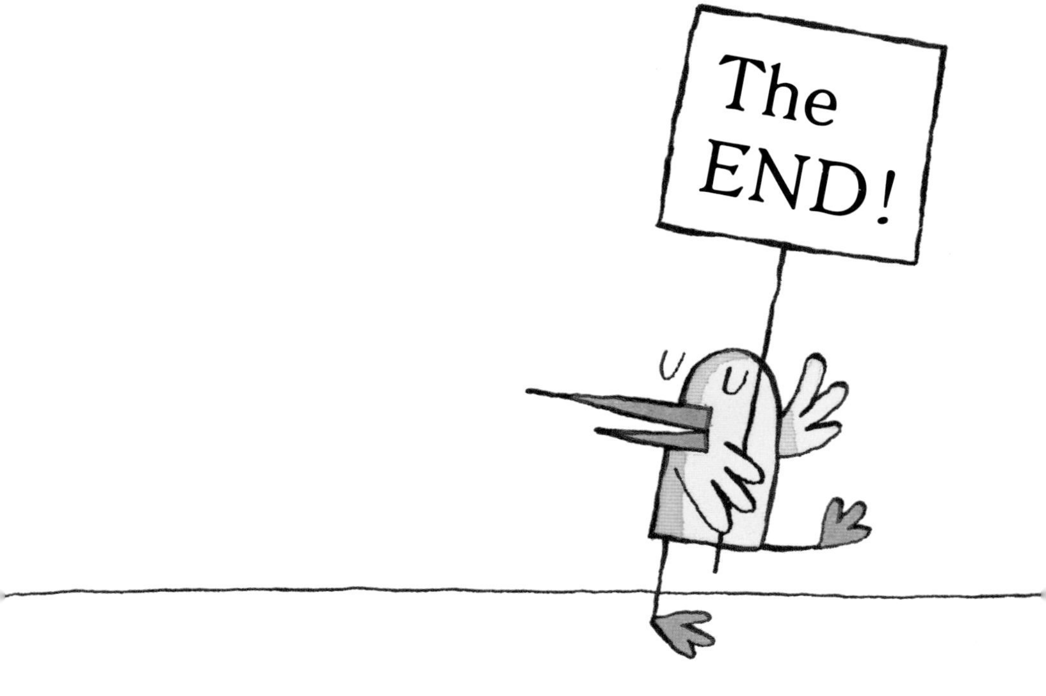
The
END!

Look, Jerry Kalback, look!
This book is for you.

First edition 2019

Library of Congress Catalog Card Number pending
ISBN 978-0-7636-7936-1

19 20 21 22 23 24 CCP 10 9 8 7 6 5 4 3 2 1

Printed in Shenzhen, Guangdong, China

This book was typeset in JHA My Happy 70s.
The illustrations were created in watercolor and ink.

Candlewick Press
99 Dover Street
Somerville, Massachusetts 02144

visit us at www.candlewick.com